T0090393

Sasquatch Rainbow School

by

Lyle L. Hanson

Cover and Illustrations by Leanna Hanson

TRAFFORD

Order this book online at www.trafford.com
or email orders@trafford.com

Most Trafford titles are also available at major online book retailers.

Printed in Victoria, BC, Canada.

ISBN: 978-1-4251-4927-7 (sc)
ISBN: 978-1-4251-4928-4 (eb)

*Our mission is to efficiently provide the world's finest, most comprehensive
book publishing service, enabling every author to experience success.
To find out how to publish your book, your way, and have it available
worldwide, visit us online at www.trafford.com*

Trafford rev. 4/16/2010

Trafford
PUBLISHING® www.trafford.com

North America & international
toll-free: 1 888 232 4444 (USA & Canada)
phone: 250 383 6864 ♦ fax: 812 355 4082

To my grandchildren, Isabelle, Cary, and Alicia.

Contents

Preface

How does one distinguish between paranormal events and coincidences? I don't know if there's a surefire way to tell. Many folks have things happen which are difficult to explain in terms of science, so this has led many to beliefs in the paranormal. In my own life, two such events have left me scratching my head - one in the late 70s, as I taught elementary students in Kirkland, Washington. The other happened January 15, 2004.

In the 70s, I had been developing a series of science units, and, one Friday, I told my wife, "I think I'll bring those units home from school in case there's a fire." To that point, I had never had a similar thought. That Sunday, it happened - a million dollar fire at the school, started by a couple of junior high boys playing with road flares. During cleanup, the following day, several parents were helping put my portable classroom back together, and one said she'd been having dreams of fires the previous week. Another parent said that her mother had called from Colorado, saying, "There's been a fire, hasn't there?" Three separate intuitive events all coalesced to that traumatic Sunday fire. Coincidence or Paranormal experiences? Who knows?

The other interesting event of this nature happened as I was writing this preface. A TV newscast announced that Seattle was set to open a Paranormal Museum, and the visual showed a still image of Roger Patterson's, now famous, filmed Sasquatch sighting in California. Again, there's something rather eerie going on here.

I must admit, I remain undecided on the question of coincidence or paranormal, so I leave it for you to decide.

For most of my adult life, I have been fascinated by Sasquatch tales. In fact, my first two Sasquatch books, SASQUATCH SUPERSTAR and SASQUATCH RAINBOW SCHOOL were both written during the mid-seventies during my elementary school teaching career. Most of my sixth-grade classes loved SUPERSTAR, and they believed, nearly unanimously, it should be published and made into a movie. But I sensed RAINBOW SCHOOL might be a bit beyond their attention spans. I felt that this second volume is probably more appropriate for older students and adults. Now, during my retirement, I decided to revise and update these two Sasquatch fantasy books.

These books are fiction, and they arise from my imagination. Little, if any, lore on Sasquatch/Bigfoot has ever been proven, conclusively. In fact, one man recently died whose family reported that he had been behind many of the enormous footprints that have been found. So, as far as I can tell, the case for Sasquatch has yet to be made. And my books do not attempt to make the case for them, either.

Because this book deals with the history of the universe and creation of human beings, I'm certain to at least raise eyebrows from religious folks who have their own beliefs about creation. This book makes no attempt to be factual, and everything except some researched areas arises from my imagination. Face it, folks, not all imagination is extinguished in elementary school. Some of us Medicare citizens still have it.

What would it be like if some space creatures were so advanced that they could film the creation of our solar system using holography? And what if they could reveal all these great stories to our civilized Sasquatch - civilized from a professional basketball career?

!

The

Agreement

A gust of late autumn wind struck Satch square on his broad nose. Most of his internal and external nasal hairs vibrated slowly, creating an annoying irritation. The Sasquatch turned over, drowsily, to face the hollow log, which still served as his peach cache. Just above him, a lean-to shelter of pine boughs shimmered in the early morning breeze.

For a few brief moments before waking fully, Satch's mind wandered back to the night, years ago, when that same hollow log had lured the giant Sasquatch into a fearful trap. He reflected on his training, which had transformed him into the most awesome superstar in professional basketball. Finally, he moved his heel back and forth as if testing his repaired Achilles' tendon severed in his final game.

Since returning to the pinewoods, he had tested it many times, running and walking around the deer trails. Every tree, bush and fallen log seemed as familiar to the Sasquatch as a person's own furniture. The forest was his rightful home, and each new day brought him a sense of deep inner peace. True, he had enjoyed his brief flirtation with fame, but his natural environment meant even more to him.

Both dark eyelids popped open together, and Satch raised himself slightly on his hairy elbows. Then he scooted out of the lean-to backwards. Quickly, he raised himself up to his full eight-foot height and increased this by another three feet with a mighty stretch toward the gray sky. He yawned deeply, drawing the clear, crisp Eastern Washington forest air into the depths of his lungs.

It was the same every morning - up at the first sign of dawn, the mighty stretch and the deep yawn. Then his part of the forest awoke with a flurry of activity. Satch began each day with a series of physical exercises, learned during his athletic training. First came the body bends. The Sasquatch raised his hands high overhead and then bent over to touch the palms flat on the forest floor. Without effort, he kept his knees straight during the entire process.

Following 100 - 150 body bends, he performed 120 sit-ups and 90 pushups. By then, his enormous 550-pound frame had shook off the chill of the cool air, and he felt alive.

He greeted his world with a mighty trumpeting bellow, "EEE --- OOO --- WAA!" In a flash, he raced off on a course through the forest known only to him.

Fifteen minutes later, he collapsed in an exhausted heap in front of his refrigerator, the hollow log. The Sasquatch shoved a hairy arm inside, up to the elbow, and clutched six peaches. Quickly drawing them out, he shoved them all into the cave, which was his mouth.

Almost immediately, the fragrant juices seeped out over his lower lip, catching on the thick mat of his chin whiskers. His eyes sparkled contentedly as he ate. Breakfast ended, as usual, with the "machine gun" act. With lips pursed into an O, Satch expelled the six peach pits with a "rat-a-tat-tat" against a tree trunk nearly 20 feet away.

After wiping his juicy chin with a forefinger and then

licking it clean, he ambled over to the edge of the forest at a vacant field. Far across the clearing, his eyes sought out the familiar sight of the Stevensons' wood frame home. Satch recalled that he'd agreed to deliver several commercial pitches for their peaches at some supermarket in return for a continuous supply of peaches. The Sasquatch sensed that the time had arrived for him to approach the Stevensons and offer to complete the agreement.

He headed across the field, noting the prickly stubs of broken weed stems on the soles of his leathery, 18-inch feet. They tickled, rather than hurt. Some of the taller weeds also tickled his hairy ankles and shins. As always, the approaching peach orchard appeared inviting to the fruit-loving animal.

Just before reaching the peach trees, Satch was startled by a strongly assertive female voice, "Well, hello, Big Fellow. I was wondering when you'd come." It was Marcie Stevenson, the new business head of the family. She'd taken on that role when her dad, Dan, had died several years earlier. Stepping between a couple of trees and into an open area, the young lady, dressed in plaid shirt and jeans, appeared completely self-assured.

Satch waved a mighty arm back and forth, shouting, "Greetings from the forest. You didn't have to worry about me not showing up. I like your peaches too much."

As the two figures approached each other, they both grinned and then shook hands. Marcie grimaced and yelled, "Ow! Ow! Take it easy Satch. You don't realize your own strength."

Quickly, Satch released his vice-like grip, and his gigantic eyes looked down, apologetically. "Gosh, Marcie, I'm really sorry. It's been quite a while since I shook hands with anyone. Guess I just forgot how. You OK, Marcie?"

"Sure," she replied, inspecting her trembling right hand, "just a few broken bones, no doubt. I'll be all right." Quickly, Marcie erased the pain from her mind and grinned, as her thoughts turned to Satch's public appearances. "Come over to the house, and we'll talk business."

The pair walked side-by-side, past the orchard, up the back steps, through the screen door and entered the kitchen. Marcie's mother, Ellie glanced up from her dish washing as the two figures emerged. She gasped as Satch nearly entrapped himself within the doorframe. His head was bent far forward, and he had to force his shoulders sideways in order to enter.

Ellie had seen Satch before, during the weeks following his capture. But her observation had been from a safe distance, with Satch secured inside the cage/trap. Satch, at that moment, seemed to fill half her kitchen. She choked back a wide-eyed scream, a combination of fright and surprise.

Ellie regained her composure, quickly, noting the relaxed look on her daughter, Marcie's face. Her grown, tomboy protector said, "Take it easy, Mom. It's just our old friend, Satch. He came over to talk business."

Satch noticed a few more age lines on Ellie's face and a few more gray hairs. Otherwise, he noted, the years had been kind to Ellie. She remained a pretty woman and even managed a brief smile as she forced herself to say, "Hello, Satch. Make yourself comfortable."

Nodding agreement, Satch replied, "Thanks, Mrs. Stevenson. This is a nice house. I'll be gentle with it."

"How about fixing us a couple cups of coffee, Mom?" asked Marcie.

Satch frowned and said, quickly, "I can't drink that stuff. Do you have any peach juice?"

"No," said Ellie, "but I can make some in my juicing machine."

Grinning broadly, Satch said, "Gee, thanks, Mrs. Stevenson."

Marcie and Satch walked into the living room, and they sat down on the couch to talk business. Marcie began by saying, "Satch, I've got a job lined up for you over at the Omak Thriftmore Market. The manager said you could come over any Saturday because that's their busiest day. Lots of shoppers coming and going all day long. He is fixing up a big platform for you and will load it up with full peach baskets."

Satch listened intently and nodded for Marcie to continue.

"I have written a speech for you. I'd like you to memorize it and, that day, stand up on the platform and recite it into a microphone and loudspeaker setup. I figure you could make the speech every half-hour and sign autographs in between times. You should draw big crowds, because we'll advertise your appearance in the Omak newspaper. Everyone around here knows about you. You were an amazing sensation when we captured you and became such a famous basketball star. Naturally, I'll expect you to eat up lots of peaches to show the people just how delicious our fruit tastes."

At the mention of peaches, Satch began drooling slightly from the corners of his broad lips. Just then, Ellie entered the front room with the cup of coffee and a tall glass of peach juice. Satch reached out, engulfed the glass and gulped the contents down with a single, "Glug!" Then he wiped his mouth with the back of his hand and emitted a loud burp.

Ellie handed Marcie her cup of coffee and returned, hastily, to the kitchen, shaking her head in disbelief. Marcie set the cup down on an end table and continued the discussion. "I've been working on your speech for some time, and it's finally polished and ready to roll. Just a minute. I'll get it."

Marcie rose and walked a few steps over to her business desk. She opened a drawer and withdrew a computer printout. "Here it is," she said, returning to the couch. "I'll read it to you. It says, 'Hi, folks. It's sure nice of you to come out to see me, today. No doubt, you are familiar with the basketball record of Satch Stevenson. I'm proud that I helped the Las Vegas Bandits win their first World Championship – also that I won rookie-of-the-year honors during my first season as a pro.

'I had to watch my diet in order to perform so well on the basketball court. One time, I got stomach poisoning from eating some junk at a carnival. So now, I always eat the world's most perfect food – peaches.

'I've been eating this delicious fruit from Peachcrest ever since I can remember. In fact, I got captured as a direct result of stealing peaches. You kids, listen to me. Never steal. I only did that because I didn't know any better. I hated spending all those months inside that cage prison. Now, I know enough to work for my peaches.

'This store has been very kind in letting me come here to visit with you great people. Just in case you would like to try a few of these succulent treats, there are lots more of them inside the store. But, please, always remember to ask for Peachcrest peaches by name. Accept no substitutes. Remember, folks, Satch and Peachcrest peaches belong together. Now, I'll be happy to sign free autographs for any of you.'"

Satch looked thoughtfully at Marcie and said, "Sounds fine to me. I can handle that. When's the day?"

"This coming Saturday – day after tomorrow. OK?"

"Sure, Marcie, that gives me plenty of time to memorize the speech. I'll return here Saturday morning. See you then." Satch engulfed the speech in his immense hand and eased himself out the kitchen door.

As he strolled lazily past the rows of peach trees, Satch thought that Marcie's proposal sounded more than fair. It would be easy, fun work in exchange for many satisfying meals. Then, too, he enjoyed the attention of humans. Many times since returning to his pine tree forest, he had daydreamed of the times when thousands of basketball fans in the Las Vegas Arena had welcomed him with screams, cheers, whistles and foot-stomping. Such responses would make any Sasquatch feel warm and proud.

Soon, Satch stepped into the weeds and grass of the vacant field. Once again, he felt the tickling, scratching sensation on his feet and legs. Part way across the field, the former basketball great recalled his inspirational antics on the hardwood court. He felt the craving for just one more Peach Tree Blast, where he leaped skyward and fired the ball downward through the hoop, often shredding the net in the process. He prepared for an imaginary Peach Tree Blast with no basket or ball.

The towering Sasquatch gripped Marcie's speech in his left hand and palmed a phantom basketball in his right. The exact sequence of moves: three long strides while dribbling the ball, a tremendous upward leap, the ball slamming through the net – all this flashed through Satch's mind a split-second before he sprang into action.

At the top of his patented leap, Satch's right arm seemed to dissolve as if all the strength drained out of it, instantly. The Peach Tree Blast disintegrated. During the brief airborne moment, Satch's silver dollar sized eyes absorbed a strange sight about a hundred feet ahead of him. He felt a tremble course through his muscular body and he grew instantly cold.

II

The

Intruders

This odd feature had been invisible to him previously because it was hidden by some taller surrounding grass. But from a height, the observant Sasquatch noticed an odd circular depression where the grass was missing or bent.

Satch's deepest instincts urged him to investigate. Most animals display strong drives to explore their environments fully. Possibly, this instinct helps them discover hidden dangers and helps them survive longer.

He approached the circle very cautiously, as if expecting a trap. Near the grassless depression, he noticed that it formed a dark brown circle, as if it had been burned. At close range, he could tell that the grass and weeds had been scorched off at ground level. It reminded him a bit of the time a portion of the forest had been burned following an electrical storm.

But this formation was most peculiar to Satch. Why was the grass burned in a perfectly circular way? He stood at the edge and stared at the area for several minutes.

Then he decided to measure the burned area. He knew from past basketball experience that his own stride measured about five feet. So he paced off the distance across the parched circle. It took exactly six steps. Quickly, Satch calculated that the circle was roughly 30 feet in diameter.

There was little to do but stroke his hairy chin in wonderment and think. At first, he questioned his own eyesight. After some vigorous rubbing of his closed eyelids, the strange area remained.

Next, he thought that some farmer might have bought the vacant field and tried to clear it of grass before planting a crop. But why in a circular pattern? It simply didn't make sense. Besides, the circle was just too exact.

At last, Satch decided that there was only one way to solve the mystery. He would stake out the burned area by moving his lean-to shelter to the edge of the forest where he could watch the field for any further developments.

After walking back into the forest, he prepared for his move. With a tremendous grunt, he tried lifting his hollow log. It wouldn't budge. It had lain on the forest floor so long that it was hard to distinguish its edges from the matting of twigs, cones and pine needles weaving a mat on the forest floor.

Satch decided to excavate the log, using his rigid fingers as a hoe. This proved agonizing work, and the Sasquatch's fingertips grew raw before the log worked loose.

His first aid technique was to clean the wounded area as best he could. For several minutes, he held the painful fingertips inside his mouth and swabbed them back and forth with his tongue. This process eased the pain.

Next, the Sasquatch bent his powerfully muscular body to the task of lifting the log. With one huge effort, the log was freed from the forest floor. He raised it high enough to rest it on his shoulder. Then he strained to pull his burden toward the edge of the forest.

Several times, he let the log fall to the ground while he caught his breath. Each new effort to hoist the log seemed to make the forest floor shake. But each time, he managed to raise it high enough to resume the trudge.

By the time he had inched the log over to the edge of the forest, Satch's face and body were drenched in sweat. It blinded his eyes and he rubbed them, strenuously, with the back of his hand. He collapsed on the ground with his head propped up slightly against the log.

Satch was unaware of dozing off to sleep, but when he woke up, he realized that there was more work to complete. It was a relatively easy task to gather broken pine branches and rebuild his lean-to. Carefully, he arranged the hollow log and branches so that his eyes could face the mysterious circle during his rest.

Following a large 12-peach dinner, Satch crawled into his bed. His eyes stayed open for a long time as the curious Sasquatch followed the crescent moon's slow, steady journey through the cloudless night sky. As darkness deepened, Satch delighted in viewing the countless sparkling stars in their fascinating patterns. Every so often, he spotted a streaking meteor and wondered what it meant.

Just as he was dozing off for the night, his keen animal senses picked up a soft buzzing sound, which mimicked distant swarming bees. He opened his eyelids and gazed up again at the night sky. As he searched for the source of the eerie sound, he noticed that the buzzing increased.

An instant later, Satch's eyes focused on a small, round orange glow high overhead. It moved fully as fast as the meteors, but every few seconds, its direction changed. This action was unlike the meteors, which seemed to follow a straight path.

Soon, the orange glow grew larger and larger until it hovered over the grassy field. Suddenly, the orange light switched to blue as the object came into clear view above Satch's head.

The Sasquatch's breathing sped up, considerably, as he spotted a circular flying object hovering just above the scorched circle in the field. The buzzing changed to a soft hum as the slightly vibrating machine stood motionless, defying gravity, at tree top level. Moments later, the object settled slowly down into the burned area. The humming stopped.

Satch trembled as his fearful eyes surveyed the sight. For a moment, he toyed with the idea of clamping his eyes together, tightly, as if to block a bad dream. But his animal curiosity finally overcame his fear. He inched his body out of the lean-to, and felt his body shake. As he faced the pulsating pale blue object, he noted that the Stevenson peach trees effectively shaded the house. The light would probably not interrupt their sleep.

Satch realized that he, alone, must face the unwanted guest. As he stood and gazed toward the light, he felt his muscles ripple, one by one. He forced his shoulders back, stuck out his enormous chest and edged, cautiously, toward the foreign glow.

After a few steps, the Sasquatch froze. He detected movement. A large silver cylinder descended from the center of the circular craft. Moments later, a group of tiny creatures emerged from an opening in the cylinder. They stood no more than four feet tall and wore shiny metallic clothes. Their bodies seemed much too small for their heads.

Almost immediately, the small men noticed Satch, for he stood within range of the blue light. They began waving, frantically, at the towering Sasquatch. To Satch, it appeared that the beings were motioning him to approach. He felt, somehow, compelled to move toward the mysterious object and the small men who beckoned him.

The hairy behemoth walked forward with cautious steps. In a strange fog, the creatures scrambled down the side of the glowing object and walked toward Satch. When they were about 10 feet away, one of the beings raised an arm. An instant later, Satch was blinded by a flash brighter than a dozen suns. He fell to the ground, quivered twice and lay dazed.

The
Abduction

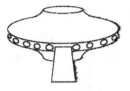

When Satch regained consciousness, his head was filled with ringing sounds, as if he were the clapper in someone's alarm clock. Several minutes later, the ringing quieted enough for him to become aware of his other senses, one by one.

First, he felt that his body had been placed on a bunk bed, or rather two bunk beds placed end-to-end. He could feel a narrow gap at the small of his back. Otherwise, the mattresses felt as comfortable as feather pillows.

Next, he heard a captor's hushed voice. Then, several others joined the talk. They spoke a foreign language in muted tones, which seemed almost soothing to Satch's aching ears. He also detected a pulsating background hum of the type he'd heard as the object landed.

At last, Satch mustered up enough courage to open his eyes. He recoiled at the sight of a tiny red skinned being bending over him. Quickly, Satch spotted the others standing nearby. In all, there were eight of the creatures, alike in every observable way except one – the color of their skin.

Satch had observed rainbows on many occasions, when the sun peeked out from behind clouds near the end of afternoon showers. These little beings displayed most of the colors of the rainbow: yellow, orange, pink, red, green, violet and blue. The eighth one, standing near the back of the group, was dark brown.

Each of Satch's captors wore a tight-fitting uniform consisting of tiny, overlapping silver plates. These outfits made them resemble fishes with shiny scales.

But their large hairless heads reminded Satch more of human types. They sported the same type of ears, eyes, noses and mouths as humans, except that their eyes appeared deeper set and their lips were as thin as pencil lines. Overall, the head shape reminded Satch of colored light bulbs.

Their feet were encased in tall black boots. They wore gloves to match. Satch estimated that they stood just under four feet tall.

"Do not be afraid, Earth Creature," said the red one. "We return to the village of Peachcrest, state of Washington, country of the United States, continent of North America and planet of Earth in order to teach you the secrets of the Universe. I am the commander of this mission. Courage is my name."

Satch trembled and asked, "But, why me?"

The little red creature stood up a bit straighter and said, "There are three reasons for choosing you. First, your species gave rise to human beings. Second, you are the only one of your species that understands language. The last, and perhaps most important reason, is that you lack the greed which is so widespread among human beings. We feel that you will share our information with other Earthlings without seeking to enrich yourself.

"We know of your unselfish basketball playing skills and your donations of large sums of money to charities. We have seen you attempt to sell products on television, and we are impressed with your basic sincerity. In sum, you are a rare breed – perfectly suited to receive the truth."

"You see," continued Courage, "we have attempted to communicate with Earthlings many times and in many ways. We have been shot at with anti-aircraft weapons and guns.

Airplanes have also attempted to shoot us out of the sky. Still, our superiors continue to order us to communicate our story. You represent our final solution to the problem."

Satch sat up on the edge of his bunk. He noticed several other beds around the outside of the compartment. Just beyond the group of colorful beings was a closed hatch. A single fluorescent lighting fixture shone brightly overhead.

"Don't try what you are thinking," the red spokesman warned. "You see, our people have long understood the technique of mental telepathy – commonly known as mind reading. For example, just a moment ago you were thinking that you would try to knock us down and escape through the hatch. That is impossible and foolish. Each of us comes equipped with the ability to create temporary mind paralysis in an individual. With a single high-energy stare from any one of us, you would be rendered completely helpless. Do not force us to act. There is no need to resist us. You will not be harmed.

"Allow me to explain our mission in greater detail. First, we are proud members of the Rainbow Race. Our home sun is Pollux, a mere 35 light years from Earth. Our planet was known as Veskin and was the fifth of seven in distance from Pollux. I say WAS because Veskin was destroyed five and one-half billion years ago by a race of warlike beings from the planetary system of the double star Boötes Epsilon, 105 light years from Earth. 5500 of our people escaped in a photon-driven space ark. Upon entering your solar system, we settled into an orbit around Venus. From this outpost, we have sent out surveillance craft, such as the one you are now inside, to help direct the fate of your planet."

Satch frowned and scratched his grizzled brow, "But how?" he asked. "How could you visit our planet from somewhere so far away? How could you look so much the same and yet show such different colored skin? How could you direct our planet's fate?"

"Earthling," said the leader, "these questions will be answered in due course. If you have eyes that can see, ears which can hear and a mind which can understand, then you may discover the secrets of eternity. We have prepared a series of cosmic lessons, and each of us here in this compartment is a skilled teacher whose goal is to guide you to the truth."

"Allow me to introduce your guides for this historic trip." Courage turned to his right and extended his black-gloved hand toward his green companion. "Nature will be your first guide."

The green one gazed at Satch with an expressionless stare. He said, "It is my task to reveal to you the development of life here on Earth. As you shall see, your species, the Sasquatches, played a very important role."

Turning next to the tiny pink creature, Courage again motioned with his hand and said, "This is Flesh – another fine instructor who will work with you."

Flesh brightened, momentarily, with a trace of a smile on his otherwise passive face. He said, earnestly, "I am an expert on human beings and will share with you some lost moments in the history of mankind."

Continuing in clockwise fashion, the red leader next pointed to the violet being, saying, "Next, meet Woe. You will find his lessons exciting, yet sad."

The violet individual, living up to his name, appeared sad as he drooped his face and said, "It is my unhappy task to describe to you the great catastrophes which have altered the history of Earth."

Turning further to his right, Courage pointed toward the bluish being and said, "Next, meet Torrent."

The one called Torrent said, evenly, "I am a specialist in a substance well-known to Earthlings – water. Even though water covers about two-thirds of the Earth and is as common as a kitchen faucet, still this precious chemical compound of oxygen and hydrogen remains little understood."

Next, in order of introduction was the orange one. Courage continued by saying, "This is Strength. You should be able to identify with him."

Miniature muscles rippled, momentarily, beneath the silver blouse of Strength. He stood ramrod straight and said, seriously, "You are my ideal type of creature because power and endurance are etched on your face. There have been numerous examples of superhuman forces throughout time. We shall experience some of them."

To Strength's left, the yellow being appeared to puff out his chest a bit in anticipation of being introduced. "This is Golden. You will find his stories very rich," said Courage.

"It is my pleasure," said Golden, "to reveal the ageless science of transforming common metals into precious substances such as silver and gold. You shall discover the secrets of the Golden Age."

Last among the group of teachers was the dark brown one. Gesturing once again, Courage said, "This is Immortality, the last of our group."

Satch noticed that Immortality's eyes seemed sunken deeper than the rest, as if they belonged to an ancient one. Aside from that, his body structure and features were identical to the rest.

The dark being said, solemnly, "I can tell that you're wondering why I look so old. Well, it might help to mention that each of your teachers is over 10 billion years old, and I am older than the rest."

Satch's huge eyes widened, in awe. He wondered if he were awake. Such hints of fantasy boggled his mind. Still, stark fear urged him to cooperate with his captors. Gradually, he began trusting the sincerity of the weird-looking ones. There was little else he could do, Satch concluded, recalling the paralyzing shock he'd received outside the spacecraft.

"I'm pleased that you have decided to cooperate," said the red-skinned leader.

"I play a dual role – leader and one of your instructors. From my extensive experience, you will learn the secrets of artificial gravity and the workings of spacecraft, such as ours.

"We call our instruction the Rainbow School," continued Strength. "It shall last several days. Each day, we must move to a different uninhabited spot. It is of vital importance that no interruptions occur. You are our first and only student. We expect you to ask questions about any aspect of these lessons which puzzle you."

Nervous anxiety gripped Satch's mind. Courage interrupted his Sasquatch thoughts and said, "You're worried about your supermarket appointment on Saturday. Please relax. Your job can wait. The Rainbow School cannot."

"Gosh!" exclaimed Satch, "I can't understand how you can know my thoughts like that!"

Courage smiled, broadly, at the compliment and replied, "It's quite elementary, as you shall see. But now, let us sleep. Before dawn, we'll zip off to our first classroom in Africa's depths."

Satch nodded, wearily, and let his huge body sink back down to rest on the miniature bunks. He felt certain that every tingling nerve in his body would prevent him from sleep. But he began snoring just as the vacant field was struck by a gust of wind from the rising spacecraft.

IV

Nature's Lesson

Satch was roused from his peaceful slumber by a steady tapping on his chest. His weary eyes opened just a crack, and he noticed Courage, the red leader, standing over him.

"Time to wake up, Earthling," said Courage with a friendly smile. "I've brought you some breakfast," he said, gesturing toward a bucket of peaches on the floor. "You seem more at ease, now, and not at all surprised that we knew about your favorite food. Do you recall dreaming about peaches last night? Your thoughts came through to all of us very well."

Satch returned the smile, nodded and answered, "Now that you mention it, I guess there were a few peaches in my dreams."

"Dig in; they're free," said Courage.

Several minutes later, Satch had downed about 14 of the fuzzy fruits. He finished by smacking his lips with a flourish and belching from the depths of his barrel gut.

"Follow me," said Courage, leading the way toward the room's only hatch. As Satch tried to stand, he found the ceiling about two feet too low. This forced him to hunch over, uncomfortably. In the narrow metal passageway outside the sleeping compartment, there was no relief. Each movement became a painful struggle for Satch. Finally, he sank to his hands and knees. This method proved easier, even though he felt rather ridiculous creeping along like a baby behind his guide.

At last, Courage unscrewed a large wheel and swung open the spacecraft door. A sudden stream of morning sunlight struck Satch in the eyes. He squinted and raised his open hand to his forehead for shade.

"Come," said Courage, leading Satch down the steps of a long ramp. Once outside, Satch felt relieved as he stood up and stretched his eight-foot frame. At the bottom of the ramp, Satch noticed that the strange spacecraft had landed in a large rectangular clearing, surrounded by very thick growths of trees and colorful plants. He heard the chattering of a variety of animals near the treetops.

The Sasquatch turned and gazed at the gleaming spacecraft. The reflected sunlight seemed to set the metal machine aglow. It stood silently, like two huge metal saucers with open ends joined. A large number of small holes dotted the midline as far around as Satch could see. Three legs spread outward from underneath, like a tripod stand. The only other structure Satch observed was the long ramp, which they had walked down moments before.

Facing the clearing, once again, Satch noticed several pieces of peculiar machinery standing about 20 feet from the spot where the ramp touched the ground. These formed a semi-circle, along with two folding chairs.

Courage marched toward the machines, with Satch following along behind. The pair stopped alongside the largest and most complicated device. "Welcome to the Rainbow School," said Courage, his eyes sparkling in obvious pride. "In a moment, Nature, today's teacher will be along. But first, let me introduce you to the classroom. We have landed in Eastern Africa, in the country known as Tanzania, at a spot near Olduvai Gorge, where human beings had their start. Today's lesson provides valuable new information concerning life on your planet Earth.

"These machines, working together, make up our holovision system. Holograms were discovered only recently by man. But it will be some time, yet, before men are able to combine them with television techniques to produce perfect three-dimensional events in color and motion. Our race discovered this process about 15 billion years ago – long before my time."

Satch stared at the complex machinery in wide-eyed curiosity, as Courage reached out and flipped a switch. The area in the center of the semi-circle came alive with a small planet, floating in the inkwell of space. Instants later, Satch saw a dark football-shaped form glide inward and stop, hovering motionless well above the globe. A hatch opened in the spacecraft and a ray, like a sunbeam, flashed down. Quickly, the planet trembled, violently, began glowing and disappeared. The dark craft paused as if inspecting the area where the planet had been. Then it slowly shrank and disappeared into the dark. Courage switched off the machine.

"Wow!" shouted the excited Satch. "That was real! That was great! Uh, what did we see?"

Courage said, "Please sit down." Satch draped the mountain which was his body onto the second chair. "What you just witnessed was the destruction of our home planet, Veskin, by the evil Trobelites of Böotes Epsilon. Fortunately, for the preservation of the Rainbow Race, we received many clues concerning their plans to destroy Veskin. As I mentioned before, 5500 of us managed to escape in a type of space ark, which is now orbiting the planet Venus.

"The scenes you just witnessed," continued the leader, "were actually recorded by our space ark as it escaped toward your planetary system. Holograms are made by illuminating a scene with light from a laser, and then recording it on photographic film. The realistic image is then created by shining a similar beam of light on the hologram. The hologram reconstructs the original light patterns. Holographic images become so realistic that they can be viewed from any angle, as can the original objects. Do you understand?"

Slowly, Satch nodded and said, "Uh-huh; I think so. The objects I saw are small but realistic duplicates of the original things. That's pretty good TV!" he said, with a broad grin.

From behind, the green Rainbow teacher approached the pair. As he reached them, Courage rose and returned to the spacecraft. Nature sat down next to Satch and encouraged him to relax and watch the coming scenes.

"What you will see," said Nature, "consists of a series of holographic reels beginning far back in time and moving toward the present. If you have any questions, please wait until the end of a reel to ask them. Ready?"

Leaning back in his chair, but with both eyes alert, Satch nodded and said, "OK."

Nature flipped the main control switch and said, "It is now five billion years ago. Your solar system is being formed in this scene."

Satch watched, spellbound, as a miniature Sun appeared center stage, revolving on its axis and moving across the classroom from left to right. At the edge of the semicircle, it disappeared and then reappeared at the far left, repeating its spinning path. Each time it crossed the stage, the surrounding space became less and less cluttered with space dust. It was as if the Sun was acting like a super magnet or vacuum cleaner. Soon, some of the larger clumps of dust began attracting each other and developing their own spinning motions. Near the end of the reel, 10 ball-shaped objects could be seen spinning and circling the moving Sun. A number of smaller objects orbited the larger ones, but these were barely seen.

Nature told Satch, "You just watched the birth of your solar system as we filmed it from space. The process took about two million years. We speeded up the pictures, somewhat." The green teacher paused, studying Satch's face.

The hairy giant grinned and said, "Yeah, somewhat!"

Nature continued, "I hope you noticed that 10 planets formed. At present, there are only nine planets in your group."

Looking surprised, Satch asked, "What happened to the other one?"

Nature appeared pleased. He smiled and said, "You have the makings of a fine student. As we suspected, the Trobelites attempted to track us and complete the extermination of the Rainbow Race. So we played a trick on them by placing a powerful radio transmitter on the sixth planet away from your Sun. We beamed messages which the Trobelites assumed were originating from our home base. They annihilated the sixth planet and left for home. Today, the remains of the sixth planet still orbit between the paths of Jupiter and Mars. Earthlings know these planetary chunks as asteroids.

"But let's get back to our main lesson," continued Nature. "Here is the next reel."

Upon touching the switch, the holovision stage was filled with the scene of a watery planet, its seas boiling, gurgling hot. Its thick atmosphere was wracked by violent thunderstorms. Lightning flashed continually on all sides. Gradually, the scene calmed and peace prevailed.

As the reel finished, Nature again spoke to Satch, "That showed the Earth during its first two and one-half billion years of life. It took that long for it to cool down enough so that we could begin our experiments."

"Your experiments?" asked Satch, becoming further entranced by his lesson.

Nature replied, "Yes, Earthling, you see, we viewed your planet as a possible new home for the remains of the Rainbow Race. Earth orbits the Sun at an ideal distance to provide excellent climate conditions for supporting life. Following the scene you just witnessed, we began seeding the Earth. At first, we found the seas still too hot to support animal life. We were overjoyed when we learned that a few types of simple water plants and animals survived and began multiplying their kind.

"It was not until the first land appeared, about 600 million years ago, that we were able to begin the garden of our dreams. Watch!" Nature paused and activated the next reel.

Satch watched, intently, as a spacecraft, identical to the one resting across the clearing, hovered over a quiet shoreline and then settled down to a landing along the beach. Two Rainbow creatures exited, each carrying a shovel and bag. Once down on the beach, they set to work digging shallow holes, reaching into their bags, withdrawing their hands, placing small plants into the holes and then covering up their roots with dirt. The next scene showed the spacecraft again hovering over the beach – a beach transformed into a shimmering, green vegetation veil.

Nature switched off the machine and said, "Yes, our planting experiment worked great. Just look around. The jungle you see on all sides contains a few of the descendants from our early experiments. Once plants began to conquer the Earth, they gave off enough waste oxygen to change the atmosphere and make it suitable for supporting land animals. Our later seeding expeditions included amphibians, insects, reptiles, mammals and birds. Many of these animal species survived until today. But some did not. Let me give you an interesting example.

"We brought along several species of giant reptiles in our space ark. For awhile, they ruled the Earth. But we discovered that these creatures had begun to wipe out other smaller groups of animals. Our solution was…well, watch."

Once again, the stage flashed to life at a prehistoric swamp. A huge meat-eating dinosaur made threatening roars with razor-like teeth slashing the filtered sunlight. Evidently, it had chased a larger plant-eater right out into the protective depths of the swamp. The predator dinosaur's shorter legs kept him within a few yards of shore. He swung his savage head back and forth in frustration at being deprived of a tasty meal.

Suddenly, the familiar saucer-shaped spacecraft zoomed in from the side. As it neared the swamp, several shots were heard, and the giant reptiles sank into the murky depths. The reel whirred and stopped.

Satch wore a look of shocked sadness, and his head and shoulders drooped.

Nature studied Satch's reactions and then spoke solemnly, "I'm sorry that you were saddened by the Earth's first big game hunt. But, you see, we felt compelled to correct our mistake. On Veskin, the giant reptiles were tamed and used as beasts of burden.

"In other words, they did much of our heavy work, just as horses, mules and oxen are used on Earth, today. To our dismay, we found that when these same animals were released to roam wild, they turned into ruthless savages, destroying many of our other transplanted animal types. The entire extinction of the giant reptiles was accomplished after several weeks of intensive hunting by all three of our spacecrafts."

"Are all three spacecrafts like the one we flew?" asked Satch.

Nature nodded and answered, "Yes, the hangar in our space ark carries two others identical to this one. But, now, I sense that you have grown weary from the morning session, so it is time for a break – what Earthlings call recess. You may explore the jungle area near the edge of the clearing, but stay within view of the spacecraft. When you see it glowing blue that means that recess is over and you are to return for your afternoon class. Your scheduled instructor for this afternoon is Flesh - the one resembling Earthling Caucasians. Now, as Earthling teachers like to say, 'Go work off some steam.'"

Satch rose quickly and raced over to the jungle's edge. His

heels dug into the dirt as a snarling leopard greeted him. Not needing that sort of trouble, Satch turned on his heels and raced in the opposite direction, looking back over his shoulder every hundred steps. With a sigh of relief, Satch noticed that the leopard lacked further interest in him.

Large animals seemed absent from the part of the jungle he entered. Once again, he breathed a large sigh. He heard the chattering of scrambling monkeys and the chorus of bird calls high in the jungle canopy crown. Quickly, Satch located a friendly-looking tree and sat down against its trunk. His attention fixed on the overhead show. Small monkeys grabbed hanging vines with hands, feet and tails. The jungle seemed in constant motion as the skittering acrobats swung every which way.

"My relatives!" exclaimed Satch. With experienced nimbleness, he began climbing the tree which he'd used for a chair moments before. Limbs bowed downward as he climbed. From ample climbing experience, Satch knew instinctively how to step safely on limbs near the point where they emerged from the trunk. Part way up, he leaned over and grabbed a vine, tested it with a sturdy jerk, found it secure and swung clear from the tree.

Instantly, the treetop chorus was stilled with a new, more fearsome call, "EEE ---OOOH --- WAAA!" It echoed and re-echoed throughout the jungle gloom.

V

Flesh's
Lesson

Throughout his acrobatic play period, Satch kept an eye on the spacecraft. Half an hour later, he spotted the bluish glow, which beckoned his return. As he walked back to the open-air classroom, he reviewed the morning's events in his mind: the destruction of Veskin, the formation of the solar system, the annihilation of the sixth planet, the seeding of life forms and the great wild game hunt which wiped out the giant reptiles. He could hardly believe what he had viewed, and, yet, it had all seemed so very real. Satch wondered what mysteries the afternoon would reveal.

As he neared the Rainbow classroom, he spotted the pink creature named Flesh sitting in a chair beside the main machine. Satch approached and took the second seat, somewhat out of breath from his recess romp.

Flesh stared at his student and said, "This afternoon, I will instruct you on one of our greatest experiments – the creation of human beings. Many human scientists believe that humans, somehow, arose from lower forms of animals by a series of accidental changes. But they are at a loss to explain the vast increase in intelligence which humans display.

"Some explain this by saying that brain size gradually increased and, along with such growth, intelligence increased.

Still, how can they explain why an elephant shows very little intelligence, but has a brain over three times as large as man's? The answer, which humans may find hard to believe, is that they got their intelligence from the Rainbow Race. Watch."

Quickly, the stage filled with the scene of a huge cliff. Giant slabs of the cliff had fallen in crisscross fashion, forming a series of natural caves. In the background, a familiar spacecraft stood waiting on its tripod landing gear. Tiny living creatures tended fires and engaged in work activities near the caves.

The holovision lens zoomed in on one group of creatures so that their features could be viewed. Satch's mouth dropped open at what he saw. A Rainbow creature heaped some small branches onto a smoldering fire. Near the cave entrance, a female Sasquatch, seated on the ground, rocked a baby back and forth on her knee. To Satch, the baby looked whitish-pink and very human. Moments later, two other Caucasian-type children darted out from inside the cave. It appeared that the two boys were playing a game of tag. Gradually, the scene dimmed.

Still very surprised, Satch asked, "Was that one of my kind – a Sasquatch?"

Flesh nodded, flashing a brief smile. Moments later, he said, "I imagined that you would be fascinated to learn that Sasquatches were the mothers of mankind, while Rainbow men were the fathers. The results of this experiment were not completely first rate.

"You see," continued Flesh, "when we crossed the huge size of the Sasquatch with the tiny size of our own people, we obtained a medium-sized human being. That was fine. When we crossed extreme hairiness with no hair, at all, we obtained a human only partially haired. That was fine, as well.

"But, the main disappointment came when we crossed very low intelligence with extremely high intellect. The result consisted of human beings with relatively large brain size, but with only mediocre intelligence. The ability of human minds was considerably limited. Even the brightest one could use only one-fourth of its brain capacity. The next part of our lesson will reveal our solution. Ready?"

Satch nodded approval and leaned slightly forward toward the stage.

The brightly lit scene revealed a yellow-skinned human male lying unconscious on a table. A tiny yellow Rainbow man resembling Golden entered the room wearing hospital garb, including a white mask. Two more Rainbow men entered, similarly dressed, carrying pans and kits of surgical tools. The first doctor reached into a kit, removed a scalpel and quickly laid back a large flap of skin from the human's skull. During this procedure a second surgeon controlled the bleeding with several clamps. The third Rainbow surgeon reached into a kit and removed a small object, like a gun. He aimed it at the human's bare skull, pulled the trigger and a fine, bright beam of light began cutting through the bone. The third surgeon traced a rectangular path on the skull and then used another instrument to pry the section of skull loose.

Next, the first surgeon replaced the removed bone section with an identically shaped thin plate of gold. Finally, one of the surgeons removed the clamps while another stapled the man's shaved scalp back in place.

Before long, the human sat up on the table and smiled at the Rainbow surgeons. They removed their masks and began helping their patient to his feet. The group exited through a side door as the scene dimmed.

Flesh gazed at Satch and explained, "You have now seen a member of the second great race of mankind, a Mongoloid, or yellow-skinned man. He originated in exactly the same way as the white children in the first scene – the cross between a Sasquatch mother and a yellow Rainbow man."

"But what were they doing to the poor man's head?" asked Satch, trembling, a bit, from the intense previous scene.

"A fine question," stated Flesh, with a trace of a smile on his lips. "Remember that I mentioned that we were very disappointed with the meager intelligence level of our human offspring? Well, the surgical procedure you just witnessed is called 'trepanning'. We have known for billions of years that gold and silver possess the remarkable ability of attracting mind particles. These tiny, invisible particles are present throughout the universe in infinite amounts. They make up the cosmic mind. This is shared, in varying degrees, by every living thing.

"Living cells absorb some of these mind particles, and these, in turn, direct conscious behavior. The brain collects more of these particles because its cells are spongier and more absorbent. Therefore, the brain is the center of most thinking and other work of the mind. However, every cell has a bit of mind ability; even a single-celled animal like the ameba is able to direct its own behavior with a primitive mind.

"When human beings mow their lawns, they don't suspect that they are dealing terrifying pain to every blade of grass. Fortunately, the grass plant survives such butchery, only to get mowed down again the next week. Most painful of all are those plants on golf greens. They get shaved almost to their very crowns. The point is that plants experience feelings that are very real."

"Do you mean that it hurts a peach tree every time I pick one?" asked Satch in a slow, worried voice.

"Not that much," laughed Flesh, "but I'm glad you're concerned about plant welfare. A peach is only a tiny fraction of the entire tree, so the feeling is similar to removing a hangnail – just a small, fleeting pain."

"Wow, that's sure a relief!" exclaimed Satch. "They're my friends, and I sure don't want to hurt them." But then the huge animal's stomach began to quake at the memory of his night raid on Dan Stevenson's peach orchard, years ago. That must have caused the peach trees a great deal of senseless pain. Satch became morose at the memories of his raid. But, he brightened a bit as he considered that he'd only broken tree limbs and not trunks. They must have survived, he thought, further relieved. He promised himself that he'd never again inflict serious damage on any plant.

During Satch's brief period of thought, Flesh studied the Sasquatch, intently, and then interrupted his thoughts by saying, "I'm sure you didn't mean to cause pain to all those peach trees you broke several years ago back at Peachcrest. Now, let's pull our thoughts back to school.

"The next series of holovision scenes feature the third original race of mankind, the Negroid. These humans also had Sasquatch mothers and brown Rainbow fathers. Like the others, they received trepanning operations in order to bring their intelligence up to an acceptable point.

"The people you'll observe in a moment," continued Flesh, were unaware that they were being filmed. They were simply practicing some of their more rigorous mental exercises. Prepare yourself for the first 'Great Science Circus', filled with action guaranteed to amaze and delight you."

Satch nodded, and Flesh flipped the projector switch. A group of five Negroid men, dressed only in skirt-like clothing, entered the stage along the shore of a large body of water – perhaps a lake. Each of them stared toward a spot about 20 feet off shore and began chanting something, which sounded like, "Rada mott! Rada mott!"

Repeating the chant with increasing force, the men pointed to a designated area of the lake. Slowly, at first, and then with increasing acceleration, a sunken tree rose toward the water's surface. It continued accelerating until it smashed through the lake's quiet surface film with an enormous sonic boom. The dripping tree seemed to apply some unseen brakes and float motionless about 15 feet above the lake.

Then, as the men pivoted their arms and index fingers in unison toward shore, the tree appeared to obey by following an invisible path. It made a gentle landing near the men just as a huge wave from the disturbance crashed into them, knocking all five backwards off their feet. For a few seconds, the wave's energy sent them reeling and sliding around on the shore. But they arose, smiling, dripping wet, shaking hands and patting each other's backs.

Flesh switched off the machine and paused a moment to permit Satch to contemplate the enormity of the scene. The Sasquatch alertly created connections between pieces of information and then asked some very intelligent questions.

"Did that trick depend on trepanning and increased mind particles?" asked Satch.

Flesh smiled, responding, "A fine guess. This trick, as you call it, is known as levitation. The task of moving inanimate matter, by thought alone, requires exceptional intellect and near-total concentration. But the results are more than worth the effort. Imagine the possibilities of such ability – mind controlling matter – the ability to move mountains without flexing so much as a muscle or relying on huge, energy-guzzling machines to accomplish the task.

"Next," continued Flesh, "you will witness a higher level of this ability – one person acting alone."

In the following scene, a Negroid male appeared. He was seated at a table inside a primitive grass hut. He faced the camera, and in this position, every mannerism could be viewed in detail. Before him on the table, rested a meal in earthenware dishes. His cup held a liquid drink. In front of the meal, a candle illuminated the man's face. He appeared to tense his facial muscles and thick veins bulged along his neck. His hands gripped the table's edge. His staring eyeballs protruded from their sockets. Slowly, piece-by-piece, kernels of rice began rising from the plate in single file. They arced toward his open mouth. The kernels entered at exactly the right speed to allow chewing and swallowing before others entered.

When the plate had emptied itself, completely, the man relaxed a minute, wiping his lips with the back of his hand. Then he resumed his intense concentration. This time, several rivulets of sweat formed miniature streams, which flowed downward across his furrowed brow.

A thin stream of liquid rose, slowly, from his cup. It eased upward into his open mouth. The stream paused long enough for him to swallow. Then it began flowing once more. The process continued until the liquid was completely gone. A complete meal had been consumed without a hand raised to help it along. As if to provide a suitable finish to the entire scene, the lit candle rose, flew straight out the window and the stage grew dark.

Satch looked down intently at Flesh and said, "I think I understand. This man had practiced the first steps of chanting and finger pointing, together with other men. He graduated to a higher level of levitation and acted without benefit of some of the beginning tasks."

"Exactly," beamed Flesh, sticking out his chest, in pride. "This advanced stage is commonly called the level of poltergeist activity. In recent years, such happenings have been dismissed as actions of so-called ghosts. But, believe me, there are no ghosts. Higher levels of mental activity? Yes. Ghosts? No.

"Now, I shall conclude today's session with a somewhat different result of trepanning," said Flesh. He turned back toward the machine and the familiar holovision hum. The entire stage looked different from any previous scene. It was dark. Several minutes passed before Satch's eyes could make out the dim scene. Then, he barely noticed a dark figure lying on his back staring upward at a sparkling, starlit sky. The man's eyes were open, as if studying the heavens in great detail.

Minutes later, the man rose and walked over to a cave, which he entered by stooping over a bit. Just inside, he picked up some equipment and then continued onward into the depths of the cave. Then, only a large circular splotch of light could be viewed. It moved in a regular arc, swinging back and forth until it stopped.

Next, a triangular light rose from the larger glob and began making glowing dots on the cave ceiling. Time after time, the triangle returned to the larger glob and then returned to the ceiling. Much later, the entire cave ceiling held glowing representations of all the star clusters – exactly as they had shone on the black night sky outside. The blackness faded, and Satch looked on in amazement as the late afternoon sun flooded the scene.

Satch looked stumped. He just shook his head.

Noting Satch's expression, Flesh said, "This one's got you puzzled, doesn't it? Well, I expected that. Since it's so dark, the details are hard to perceive. So I'll explain. You have witnessed another benefit of trepanning – eidetic, or photographic, memory. This human studied the stars for a short while and then retreated to his cave to paint them on the ceiling exactly as he'd observed them. He used luminous, glow-in-the-dark, paint in a bucket, which was the large glowing disc you saw. The smaller triangular point was simply a paintbrush tip.

"I hope you noticed the exact duplication of the outside star clusters reproduced on the cave ceiling. From memory, he painted about a thousand tiny points of light in their exact relationship and distance from one another. That's eidetic memory!"

"That's amazing!" blurted Satch, in awe. "I once memorized

English and thought that was quite a feat. Of course, I never learned to spell it. But, maybe if I'd had some of that...I-did-it..."

"Eidetic," corrected Flesh.

"Eidetic memory," continued Satch, "why then maybe I could have even learned to spell it."

Flesh chuckled, briefly, before his dignity as teacher caught him up short.

The pink teacher said, "Now it's time to enter the spacecraft for dinner with the others and then off to bed. Sunrise will bring another very big day for us – much more to learn."

Satch pleaded, with a hang-dog expression, "Aw, gee, Mr. Flesh. Couldn't you just let me sleep outside under those beautiful stars you taught me about? I'd be good and not wander off. Please?"

Flesh appeared unprepared for such a proposal. He paused, considered all of its aspects, and then nodded approval. "While you're out here," the teacher added, "be sure to try out your eidetic memory by learning all the stars. I'll bring you a bunch of peaches to keep you company."

Satch grinned, broadly, and said, "Thank you for trusting me. Just don't give me some sort of star test in the morning." The chuckling Sasquatch turned away from his teacher and ambled toward the jungle's edge.

As he approached the dark shadows of the dense vegetation, Satch turned and faced the spacecraft. It pulsated with a soft, blue light. He shook his head, back and forth, several times as if disbelieving the events of the past 24 hours. Then he turned and headed into the jungle.

Quickly locating several downed branches and vines, Satch arranged a crude shelter. As he inched himself inside to rest for the night, his keen eyes noted an approaching shadow.

"Here is your dinner," announced Flesh, pausing beside the reclining Sasquatch. The Rainbow man placed a half pail of peaches near Satch's head. Then he added, "Eat well. We leave just before dawn. We'll wake you."

The tiny space man saluted and then turned to leave the jungle gloom.

Satch called after him, "Thank you, Mr. Flesh. I'll try to be ready soon after you wake me."

Following the juicy peach meal, Satch felt his hairy, muscular back adjust to the contours along the jungle floor. He felt a twinge of fear ripple through his body as he wondered if he'd ever again see his Peachcrest home. The chattering sounds of the jungle creatures soon lulled him to sleep. Quickly, that portion of the jungle rocked with a rasping, quaking chorus of Sasquatch snores.

VI

The Team
Teachers

A rivulet of drool eased downward from the corner of Satch's mouth. A cool jungle breeze struck the moisture, causing a chilling effect. Satch's chin and lips began shivering in an effort to still the subtle sensation. He wiped his chin with the back of his hand. Moments later, his eyes popped open and they began adjusting to the dark. He turned his head toward the clearing and spotted a waving light, like a lantern or flashlight. The spot grew brighter as his eyes followed its approach.

Soon, three Rainbow men stood surrounding the Sasquatch's head. One of them carried a lantern, which glowed like a noonday sun. Satch could easily identify their colors – violet, orange and blue. The Sasquatch raised a hand to shade his eyes from the light, frowning and squinting at the same time.

Satch thought to himself, "Oh, boy! Who are they? I can't even remember their names. So much for eidetic memory."

"Good morning, Earthling," replied the orange one. He displayed his mind reading ability by saying, "I can tell that you've forgotten our names. Don't worry, you're only human – or almost." Together, the trio chuckled at the joke.

"Recall that my name is Strength," said the orange spokesman, "and my colleagues are named Torrent and Woe." Strength pointed first toward the blue one and then to the

Violet one. "We have been assigned as your team teachers for the coming day. Our stories fit together, exactly, like the pieces of an Earthling jigsaw puzzle. Our instruction will move back and forth between the three of us until you receive the total picture of our important roles in the history of Earth.

"Now," continued Strength, rippling his chest muscles against the shimmering metallic space suit, "let us assure you that you will be returned to your home soon, unharmed. You worried about that, last night, before falling asleep. Our only purpose consists of educating you. We expect that you will become knowledgeable about important events, which have shaped this planet's past. In return for such knowledge, we ask only that you share these secrets with your fellow Earthlings. In sum, you, the learner, must become the most respected teacher on Earth."

Satch winced at the implications of Strength's words. Plaintively, he asked, "But what if they won't listen to me? After all, I'm only a Sasquatch and not even one of them, I mean, not even a human being."

Strength smiled at Satch, reassuringly, and said, "Do not fear. Many, many humans are ready to learn the truth. Please remember that to them you are a superstar. You have already proven that on the basketball court."

Three pairs of Rainbow eyes focused solemnly on Satch as Strength continued, "As a matter of fact, your fellow humans cannot afford to ignore your messages. To do so would lead to the destruction of their world. Now, follow us. In Egypt, we must spend our day."

The three Rainbow beings waited as Satch rose, stretched and then performed a few warm-ups. The unusual foursome then walked back to the spacecraft and climbed the ramp.

At the craft's entrance, Woe, the violet one, turned to Satch and said, "You will be permitted to ride with us in the

Flight Control Cabin during this trip. Follow us."

Satch trailed the others through the tiny sliding hatch and immediately began creeping along the passageway. Soon, they reached a ladder and climbed upward through several hatches. At the ladder's upper end, the spacecraft seemed to open like a yawning whale.

Inside, Satch was dazzled by the complex array of dials, levers, switches, computers, radar screens and other gleaming controls. Strength and Woe walked over and sat down in padded chairs in front of the elaborate console.

Torrent, the blue one, said, "I'll let the three of you prepare for our journey." Then he lowered himself down the ladder and disappeared into the depths of the spacecraft.

Satch lowered himself into the vacant third chair and located a lever which extended the back and lowered it into a slightly higher than horizontal position, much like a dentist chair. Normally, the padded chair offered ample comfort, but for Satch, it was too small. His enormous, muscular body extended over each side of the chair.

One of the Rainbow astronauts pushed a button which raised a retractable panel revealing a 180-degree, rectangular, curved windshield. Moments later, the faint background hum increased. The soft, blue exterior lighting changed to orange and then to green. Both busy astronauts adjusted the controls.

As the craft lifted off, Satch was surprised by the lack of movement sensation. During his basketball days, he'd ridden in many elevators and flown on many planes. Always, he'd experienced a heavy sensation in his stomach pit. But, just then, as the spacecraft lifted off very quickly, his eyes saw the ground falling away, but his stomach said, "No motion." For all his body felt, Satch could have been watching the Earth zip by on television. None of the usual discomforts materialized, such as taking a sharp turn in a speeding car.

Speeding onward, Satch watched the sky gradually brighten with glimpses of dawn. Below, he noted the sharp boundary between green vegetation and tan desert. Soon, the spacecraft hovered in mid-air for a moment and then began to settle gently toward the ground.

Suddenly, the cloudless dawn was cut off from Satch's view as the spacecraft lowered itself into the darkness of a vault and came to a noiseless halt. Satch peered upward intently through the windshield as a gigantic metal door slid shut, gradually cutting off the rays of friendly sunshine. The entire vault seemed to pulsate through a range of shimmering colors as the spacecraft's propulsion system gradually slowed.

At last, the craft's pale blue resting lights flooded the scene. Satch glanced across the cabin at Woe and asked, "Where are we?"

Woe completed a series of parking control checks, turned toward Satch and answered, "We have landed in a secret hangar near the Great Pyramid in Egypt. From here, we will walk through an underground corridor and enter today's classroom – the pyramid, itself. At this very moment, my colleagues are preparing the teaching machines. Come."

Strength and Woe led Satch through the spacecraft exit and down the ramp. The trio began their march down an enormous hallway, evidently carved from solid rock. Near its right angle ceiling, the walls contained rows of indirect light. Satch's built-in sensing apparatus, his hairy coat, detected a cool dampness seeping through the smoothly carved rock walls.

After a lengthy hike, the hallway ended at a much smaller rock stairway. Once again, Satch struggled to climb through a space obviously designed for normal-sized humans. Several turns in the stairway nearly caught Satch in their narrowness. At the top, the stairway opened into an expansive, cave-like room.

The room seemed perfectly squared. However, its floor,

walls and ceiling were constructed of massive rectangular blocks of stone fitted together so perfectly that Satch could not prevent himself from commenting, "These huge stones are carved so perfectly, I doubt if even a baby Sasquatch hair could fit between any of them."

Directly in the center stood the holovision classroom, arranged with four chairs – one of them already occupied by Torrent, the blue Rainbow instructor. The three others joined him and sat down.

All three Rainbow teachers gazed at Satch, as Strength began the lesson. "You have learned about some of our efforts to create a human race of mental giants here on Earth. These efforts showed signs of success, for a while. Many humans became able to move or lift huge objects through mind power, alone. But, in order to construct massive buildings out of stone, such as this pyramid, it became necessary to re-design humans in other ways.

"This was done by implanting a miniature laser in the portion of the brain which previously served no function. In effect, we made use of vacant brain space. But, through time, this secret also was lost. Today, human brains, once again, display this wasted trait.

"The small lasers could be turned on and off at will, using the excess mind particles to serve as a triggering energy source. The effects? Well…watch."

Strength flipped the holovision switch. A scene resembling a modern granite quarry filled the stage. A group of human workmen busied themselves in a remarkable way. Their eyes stared at the rock cliffs. Soon, one after another, intense light beams blazed forth from their eyes, inscribing square shapes stacked on top of each other. The piercing rays cut, instantly, into the solid rock wall, as if it were made of cheese. A worker, high atop the cliff, produced an inside cut and the top block fell free to the ground.

In a similar manner, the rest of the cubes tumbled freely to the ground. Next, each man stood near his own stone block, and in masterful concentration of laser sculpting, worked the stones into perfect spheres.

As the holovision scene faced, Strength spoke, proudly, "Now, that's real mind power. Do you agree?"

Satch continued staring ahead at the stage and muttered, "Gosh! I couldn't do that, Mr. Strength."

"You could, if you were built right," replied Strength, smiling at his student.

Briefly, Satch turned pale (as pale as a hairy Sasquatch can get), as he digested his teacher's words. "Now, wait a minute," he said. "That wasn't part of the deal. You said I'd be a student – not a patient. Don't you alter me"! Satch tensed his muscular frame and glared at Strength.

"Whatever you say, Earthling," said Strength. "We shall honor your wish. But, just remember that, should you choose, such powers are easily available through us."

"You can have them!" snapped Satch, growling slightly for emphasis.

"Fine," agreed Strength. "Now, let us continue. I suppose you're wondering why all those men made those stone balls, which were eight to 10 feet in diameter."

"Well, yes, it did cross my mind," said Satch, regaining his calm. "It seems like a rather silly waste of energy. I suppose you'll tell me they played marbles with them."

"Why, how did you know?" asked Strength, looking pleased at his pupil's insight. "Remarkable logic, Earthling. Actually, the stone spheres were used in a training game called Giant Kiss. Moving objects by mental energy alone requires extensive skill. Watch."

In an instant, the stage sprang to life with the scene of a gigantic marble game. Satch judged that the ring enclosing five of the huge spheres covered a diameter of about 100 yards. Two humans stood silently outside the ring behind their own spheres. One man began staring at his "shooter". It rolled effortlessly toward its nearest neighbor, but missed by a couple of feet. The first man hung his head in shame. The second man took his turn and found that his aim was more accurate. Each shot "kissed" the target ball dead center and sent it rolling out of the ring. The second player continued clearing the playing area until he finished the game in triumph.

Strength turned off the machine and told Satch, "Such games were mere warm-ups for the much more exacting task of building tremendous structures like the one you are now inside."

Satch frowned and asked, "But why would anyone want to build something this big?" As he finished the question, Satch spread his enormous arms apart, as if attempting to span the spacious room.

"A fair question," answered Strength. "I'll let Woe answer it."

The violet being assumed the lead, instantly, saying, "We thought we had built a rather impressive human race. They could move mountains, literally, with their minds. But it turned out that something in their nature filled them with aggression and greed. Perhaps, it was their animal start. Whatever the cause, the Rainbow Council met and evaluated their experiment at length.

"There existed a sharp difference of opinion regarding our course. One faction felt that the human race should be completely wiped out. The other group felt that it was too soon to judge the results of our experiment – that more time was needed, rather than drawing conclusions in haste.

"The result was a compromise. We decided to select a few of the more intelligent and humane individuals, show them how to preserve their great knowledge and protect themselves inside giant fallout shelters – the pyramids."

Woe stopped talking and turned his attention to the holovision machine. The stage lit up and a crowd of humans listened as a Rainbow man addressed them from a small mound of soil. "You are the chosen ones," he said, "we have hand-picked each of you men and women to carry on the human race. In order to survive, you must follow our directions to the word. You must build a giant fallout shelter, which shall be called the Great Pyramid. Other pyramids must be patterned after the first.

"The prototype pyramid shall be constructed of massive stone blocks, each weighing between two and one-half and 10 tons, with slabs lining passageways weighing over fifty tons.

"The plans for this structure must be committed to memory, soon. The pyramidal dimensions will provide exact mathematical relationships concerning the Earth's size and weight, locations of continents, days in the year, location of the Equator and an airshaft shall point directly toward the North Star.

"The base of the Great Pyramid, and the others, shall be built on solid bedrock, making it secure from any shock waves. Two airshafts, reaching outlets at 220 and 340 feet above surface level, shall prevent water from entering even during a severe tidal wave. The smoothly polished outer limestone casing will insure that objects striking the structure will slide harmlessly down to the ground.

"The pyramidal shape, itself, will ensure preservation of food. Twenty thousand alabaster jars containing provisions must be placed one-third of the way up from the base. Focused cosmic energy will prevent spoilage of the food. Now, I shall demonstrate the construction task."

The Rainbow teacher selected four humans to assist him. Quickly, they strapped backpacks onto themselves. The leader pressed a button activating an intense air jet. He whizzed upward with a whooshing sound and then hovered, motioning the humans to come. One by one, they lifted off the ground, and the crowd watched in awe as the airborne workers flew off toward the horizon and disappeared from view.

The milling crowd waited, excitedly, for 15 minutes. A mighty cheer welled skyward at the sight of five workers sailing back toward the crowd. Each levitated a perfectly-shaped block of stone above and slightly ahead of them in the air. They landed and stared the blocks down gently to the ground, side by side. The holovision stage went dark.

Woe told Satch, "After memorizing copies of the plans, a total work force of 20 men working only during daylight hours constructed the Great Pyramid within a month. Similarly, the other pyramids were built in the next couple months. When all was prepared, the chosen ones entered to safety, and we began the next phase."

Woe switched on the teaching machine. Planet Earth floated in space, spinning slowly, but evenly. A spacecraft approached but remained a considerable distance away. Then a narrow, yet intense, flash emerged from the craft. Just above the Earth's atmosphere, the flash erupted into an enormous mushroom cloud, which jolted the Earth to one side, tipping it on its axis. A rain of fire engulfed the Earth on its exposed side. The picture dimmed.

A new hologram picture faded in. A wooly mammoth, still chewing some flowers, plunged to its knees, frozen solid by an instant decrease in temperature. A tidal wave from a raging sea crashed over the beast and encased him in a sheet of ice.

Yet another picture replaced the icy scene. This one revealed a lonely pyramid withstanding battering attacks by hurricane-type winds, flying stones and later by tidal waves crashing against it. Soon the scene calmed and the pyramid stood, silently, unharmed amid the surrounding rubble at its base.

Torrent, the blue Rainbow teacher, continued the lesson by telling Satch, "The chosen ones survived the holocaust. All other humans were erased. In effect, we gave our experiment a chance to straighten out its earlier faults. Our blast rocked the entire Earth and moved it into a new orbital position around your Sun. It also tilted the Earth, causing your modern seasons. Due to shifting closer to your Moon and farther from your Sun, Earth's year increased from 360 days to 365 and one-fourth days.

"Areas near the poles, formerly warm and habitable to many life forms, became icy wastelands. In fact, entire cities still lie buried, today, beneath the polar icecaps. Vast areas of the Northern Hemisphere were covered with ice sheets, which remained for millions of years.

"The chosen ones," continued Torrent, "were instructed to begin life anew in a distant land known as Atlantis. In those days, Atlantis formed a sizable island continent in the Mediterranean Sea, in the area of present-day Crete."

Torrent switched on the next scene. A magnificent land appeared, crowned by palaces, which sparkled brightly from their outer casings of silver and gold. These were surrounded by circular stonewalls and intricate networks of man-made canals. In many areas, lush greenery provided a bountiful variety of vegetables and fruit.

Cargo ships entered and exited the canals to the nearby sea. Chariots pulled by horses along thoroughfares added to the busy atmosphere. Everywhere, this land of plenty appeared too perfect to be real.

The scene faded, and the three teachers stood up as if following some prearranged signal. "Lunch time," said Woe. We've prepared a peach shortcake for you."

"And a very special recess period," added Torrent, with an impish grin.

"Then back to your studies," said Strength, seriously,

reminding Satch of the immense importance of what he must learn.

Woe walked quickly over to a cardboard box lying next to the holovision control unit. He opened it and took out a golden brown cake, a metal bowl, some plates and some spoons. Holding the cake in front of his chest, the Rainbow being stared at the dessert. Two fine beams of light flashed from his pupils, cutting the rectangular cake into two halves. In like manner, he cut one of the halves into three smaller pieces.

Next, the pieces were placed on four plates and covered with peach sauce from the metal bowl. Woe handed Satch the half cake, which extended over the sides of his plate. The Rainbow teachers each took one of the smaller pieces.

His teachers watched the Sasquatch in amusement as he lifted the peach shortcake from his plate to his mouth and devoured it in four quick chomps. Several cake crumbs clung to the wiry whiskers around Satch's mouth. He picked these off, one by one, and ate them, too.

After all four finished eating, Torrent told Satch, "Now for your exercise period. We have prepared something special for you – an activity, which should prove exciting for a creature of your athletic instincts. We call it the Pyramid Skid. But first, follow us."

The teachers led Satch over to an air vent. Instantly, the Sasquatch felt weightless, and he flew headfirst right up the vent. Satch gasped for breath, but he was so terrified that the air caught in his throat. Sunlight pierced the shaft from above. It grew brighter as Satch neared the opening in the pyramid's outer casing.

Gradually, his speed decreased until he stopped, just as the upper half of his body cleared the vent. Squinting in the bright sunlight, Satch extended his powerful arms to each side and hoisted himself out onto the pyramid's steeply sloping side. He looked out and down. He trembled at the enormous distance to the ground.

Satch swayed a bit, dizzy from the sight of the ground over 200 feet below. His knees trembled, and he pressed his back against the gigantic stone structure, bracing both heels at the corners of the vent. Seconds later, Torrent flew out the opening right between Satch's legs.

"Don't be alarmed, Earthling," said Torrent. "This sport may leave you breathless, but under our supervision, it is completely safe."

Satch stood petrified, afraid to look up or down, his frightened eyes staring out into space over the River Nile. His knees were mush.

Torrent said, "Up you go!" Once again, Satch felt his body rise in weightless flight as his teacher directed him upward to the pyramid's tip. He came to a standing rest on a small flat stone, right at the very top. As he touched down, a tremendous surge of energy coursed through his body, causing every one of his bristly hairs to point skyward. His arms flew upward, straight out overhead, and his frightened eyes saw flashes of lightning-like energy pulses leap from his fingertips.

Surprisingly, the mighty Sasquatch felt no more fright. In fact, he experienced the familiar sensation of joy, which he'd discovered upon entering the basketball court as a superstar.

Torrent flew up beside Satch and began concentrating on the Nile River in the distance. As if obeying the Rainbow being's silent command, the river formed a swirling waterspout. It rose higher and higher into the air. The spout began arcing toward the pair, high atop the giant pyramid. A few feet below them, the water splashed down against the pyramid side.

"Now slide!" commanded Torrent, looking up brightly at Satch. Obediently, the Sasquatch hesitated, crouched and then leaped into the cascading stream of water, landing on his seat with a soggy splash. The stream created a slick surface down the pyramid's side. Satch stared wide-eyed as the ground rushed upward at him with increasing speed.

"This is the end!" he thought. Just before he hit the ground, he noticed Strength standing at the base to one side of the descending stream.

A split-second before meeting a crushing death against the ground, Strength levitated Satch and swung him gently upward through the air toward the pyramid's tip. Again, Torrent directed his path down the swift waterfall. Satch made two complete cycles before catching his breath. By the tenth trip down the steep slope, the Rainbow teachers noted a broad smile of enjoyment on Satch's face. He looked like a kid riding the Kamikaze or the Gravitron Thriller at a carnival.

After about 30 Pyramid Skids, Strength levitated Satch gently down to the ground. As their eyes met, both teacher and pupil burst into deep, rollicking peals of laughs. Satch doubled over and rolled around on the sand, mixing laughs and gasps. Then he stretched out his giant frame and felt his damp hair indent the soft sand. He relaxed with half-open eyes. His mouth curled upward in a contented smile.

A short while later, the three teachers roused the dozing Satch. He looked up at the Rainbow instructors and said, "Boy, those skids were scary, but tons of fun!"

"Yes, as we always say, they do have their ups and downs," said Woe, with a trace of a smile on his face. "We thought you'd enjoy a little fun. Students get restless and stop listening if they have to sit quietly in class too long. But, now, the afternoon schedule is set to start. Come."

The group entered the pyramid once again – this time following a set of steps leading downward and then angling upward. In the large gallery, the teaching machines waited silently, just as the teachers had left them. The four sat down again in their previous chairs.

Torrent resumed his discussion, "Now, please recall that our lesson concerned a great island continent, Atlantis, to which the survivors of the first holocaust escaped. The chosen people lived in brotherhood for several generations, and the Rainbow Council was very pleased. But, gradually, memories of the earlier catastrophe dimmed. The young Atlanteans forgot about the extermination of their ancestors. They, too, began acting in evil ways.

"So, once again, the Rainbow Council debated the problem. This time, the Council decided to act even more severely and exterminate the human race. Please focus your attention on the stage."

Satch shifted a bit in his chair and leaned forward toward the scene of a group of Rainbow men busily at work. They held portable devices in their hands. As they aimed the machines straight downward, high-pitched whines filled the air. The solid rock appeared to melt and disintegrate beneath their feet. Satch thought they must be drilling for some precious ore. Once, he'd watched tunnel drilling on TV. This was similar, except no rock debris was left behind.

The Rainbow workers progressed with startling speed. Down, down they traveled, never pausing to rest. Within five minutes, Satch estimated that the workers had descended 100 vertical feet, creating a 10-foot diameter circular shaft. At last they stopped, stood upright and floated back up to the top.

Torrent spoke as the scene dimmed. "That," he said, proudly, "was a fine demonstration of some of our advanced machines – thermal drills. They are powered by miniature atomic reactors. A graphite heating element energizes the wolfram drill tips. They leave no waste material because they melt the rock through which they bore, pressing it against the walls, where it hardens as it cools.

"Now, you were thinking that we were searching for

precious ores. Wrong. Please recall that the Rainbow Council had decided to exterminate mankind, due to their increasing evil ways. So the shaft you saw dug became the container for the largest underground nuclear explosion on Earth. Watch."

Once again, the stage contained the group of Rainbow workers near the recently dug shaft. They turned their attention to a large nearby crate. As they stared at the metal retaining straps, their laser beam eyes incised vertical lines through them and the retainers fell to the ground in pieces.

The crate sides flipped onto the ground, revealing a large black machine with several switches and dials. One of the Rainbow workers stepped forward and appeared to turn a dial and flip a switch. Then he stepped back and the group concentrated on levitating the dark machine into the equally dark shaft. Next, the Rainbow workers levitated themselves upward through the sky to enter a spacecraft, which had appeared from the blackness of the void. The craft rose and disappeared from view.

Satch felt a layer of sweat stream out across his face. His entire body tightened, as if defending itself against an approaching doom. Moments later, the Earth shrank as if the holovision camera moved back a safe distance to avoid the shock.

Then, it happened – a three-minute blast so enormous that it rocked the Earth. A gigantic mushroom cloud was accompanied by intense light. Satch covered his eyes with a trembling palm and felt pangs of sorrow as tears squeezed past his eyelids.

At last, the light dimmed enough for Satch to remove his protective hand. He squinted at the sight of the mighty continent of Atlantis slowly sinking beneath angry tidal waves. Huge clouds of reddish dust hung menacingly over the scene. Satch saw terrifying walls of seawater lash every Mediterranean seacoast and even rush outward to rock the Atlantic Ocean with its enormous force.

As the scene ended, Torrent beamed and said, "That performance was my best! Very little is left of the mighty Atlantis, today. Just a couple of small islands near Greece."

"Yes," interrupted Woe. "You put on a spectacular show, and it almost worked."

"What…what do you mean ALMOST?" spluttered the nonplussed Torrent. "D…Did you see the total destructive force of my tidal waves? Nothing could withstand their awesome force!"

"True," answered Woe, "quite true that your waves were the greatest ever. But, I'm sad to relate to this Earthling that our efforts were in vain."

"But why?" asked Satch, frowning in puzzlement. "Could any living thing survive that blast? I don't see how."

Satch's third teacher chimed in, "It came as a surprise to us, too," said Strength. "We thought we had terminated mankind. We were wrong. We failed to consider that Atlantis was a nation of sailing men. Some of them and their families were away from home during the blast. When they returned to Atlantis and found it destroyed, they sought refuge in other parts of the world. So our explosion, which equaled 2,000 hydrogen bombs, did not completely eliminate mankind. New civilizations arose in Egypt, Sumer, Mexico, Central America, South America and Greece."

Satch gazed down at Strength and said, solemnly, "I'm pleased that humans survived. Want to know why?"

"Of course," answered Strength, although he had already anticipated Satch's thoughts.

"Well," said Satch, measuring his words carefully, "if they hadn't survived, I never would have learned to speak or play basketball."

The three Rainbow teachers paused, stared at each other and then shook their heads. Strength replied, "Are those things so great compared to what we've taught you? I feel hurt. We have been revealing the secrets of the universe to you and you can only speak of learning a language and playing a childish game."

"I don't mean to sound ungrateful," said Satch, "but if I hadn't learned a language, then I could never understand all of your secrets. Right?"

Woe said, "I hadn't thought of it that way before now. But you're exactly right. Without your civilizing experiences, our Sasquatch Rainbow School would never have been launched. So I can see your point of view. But from our standpoint, we have become mightily perturbed.

"We gave birth to man, offered him our advanced technology and even trained him in brotherhood. Yet our experiments have met with little success. Humans seem unable to free themselves from the concept that might makes right – a notion, no doubt, inherited from their Sasquatch ancestors. You are an unusual Sasquatch, gentle and peaceful, and I mean no offense toward your kind. Perhaps it was our own fault. We sought to increase our offsprings' size, without due regard for the animal shortcomings of the new human types."

Satch flashed a glare of anger and shot back, "Shortcomings? My ancestors didn't ask for your experiments, did they? I'm sure they weren't exactly overjoyed to discover that their offspring turned out to be almost hairless freaks. As for shortcomings, animals don't have such things."

Strength looked up at his student and replied, "None, except that they can't think. Their behavior is programmed from birth – controlled entirely within their every cell. Their brains serve very little purpose, aside from directing their responses."

"Well, what good is thinking," argued Satch, "if you end up figuring out how to lie, cheat, steal, kill and other bad things?"

"A fine question," said Strength, smiling up at Satch. "As we shall see in tomorrow's lesson, thinking doesn't need to lead to that. Now, you've experienced a very long day. I'm sure you are hungry and tired. Would you like to sleep inside the spacecraft or outside under the stars?"

Grinning broadly, Satch said, "Are you kidding? My bed partners are the stars."

"Ours too," replied Strength, "ours too. Here, take this present with you," he added, handing Satch a cake-sized box.

As the Rainbow teachers led Satch through the complex stairways and corridors to the Great Pyramid's outside, the Sasquatch's eyelids hung heavily, and he nearly nodded off to sleep while walking. Once outside, he draped his ponderous frame of hairy muscles across the ground with his head propped up against the base of the pyramid. He barely noticed the glorious display of starlight and completely forgot about the box, which he'd set down on his stomach. In a moment, the cool Egyptian plains were rocked by the staccato rasp of Sasquatch snores.

VII

The
Golden Age

During the night, Satch dreamed of his Peachcrest home, the feel of the sharp pine needles under his body and the fresh smell of the trees. He felt something press against his face and decided that his dreamtime was done. He opened one eye just a crack and noted a Rainbow man stooping over him, pressing a finger against his facial hair. Satch felt a great craving for food and reached out for the box, which still rested on his middle.

With agile finger action, Satch opened the box and, moments later, a scrumptious aroma wafted its way up his nose. He reached inside the box, lifted out a large bowl and tipped it forward to his lips. A succulent peach Jello slithered down his cavernous gullet, like a snake sliding down its hole.

Afterwards, he set the bowl aside and looked up at the Rainbow man. The first rays of dawn brought just enough light for Satch to identify the color of his visitor. He was the yellow one.

"I hope you slept well," said Golden. You certainly ate well, it seemed."

"I slept well," replied Satch, "but not long enough. You guys seem intent upon waking me up while it's still nighttime. Why can't you let me sleep in until it's completely light outside?"

"Because," said Golden, still bending over the reclining Sasquatch, "we must fly during the dawning hours to avoid being seen by human types."

"But why?" persisted Satch. "Why should you care if humans see your spacecraft or not?"

"There are many reasons," answered Golden, patiently. "For example, every time one of our spacecrafts has been spotted, it is dismissed by your U.S. Air Force as swamp gas, ball lightning, weather balloons, Venus, hallucination or hoax. We're tired of being the subject of an elaborate cover-up. We're proud of our spacecrafts. It is a continual insult to find ourselves treated as if we don't exist.

"Of course, we understand that your officials want desperately to avoid panic, which they feel would occur should the truth about us become known. Anyhow, we're unhappy over the bad press, the lies about us and the ridicule that we've endured. So the plan is always to move during the times of least human activity. Sometimes we slip up, but always we try to move, unnoticed.

"There may come a time when we are able to move freely throughout Earth's atmosphere, but that depends on you."

"Depends on me?" shouted Satch, angrily. "Why does everything always depend on me? I am just one solitary Sasquatch and not even human!"

Golden replied, "I thought we covered that with you at the start. We decided that we couldn't reveal our story to humans, directly, because their greed would help them exploit the facts for their own monetary gain. You are the only creature alive that understands human language without having human deficits. Now come, we are late."

Slowly, Satch lifted his body onto his feet and followed Golden across the sand. At the open hangar, they climbed down a ladder to the floor and ascended to the door of the spacecraft.

When given the choice by Golden of driving or sleeping, Satch chose to doze. Inside the sleeping quarters, he draped himself over a couple of bunks. Soon, he began dreaming of his forest home. He didn't hear the hum of liftoff or see the soft glowing lights, which changed color with the craft's increasing speed – nor did he care.

Half an hour later, the spacecraft floated down effortlessly and hovered over a shimmering, blue lake. Tiny wavelets reflected the early morning sunlight like gleaming gems. Then the craft swung over toward shore and settled to Earth among some scrub brush high on a South American plateau. Several Rainbow men roused Satch from his peaceful second sleep.

They explained that the craft had landed at Guatavitá Lake on the Bogotá Plateau in the country of Columbia, South America. Because the elevation was 7500 feet above sea level and the air was always crisp, they urged Satch to pull on some clothing, which they'd obviously tailored especially for him. When dressed, Satch resembled the mythical logger, Paul Bunyan, with blue jeans and plaid, woolen shirt.

Two Rainbow men, Golden and Immortality, led Satch down to the ground. Soon, several others carried various items of equipment down the ramp and busied themselves setting up the classroom.

Meanwhile, Satch looked around. Flat lands extended on all sides of the lake to a distance of about 10 miles. Beyond, the plateau seemed enclosed by a solid ring of snow-capped peaks. The chill morning breeze flowed down across the lake from the mountains beyond, waggling the Sasquatch's facial hair. Satch noted a pair of huge vultures circling overhead.

Soon, Golden and Immortality motioned Satch to join them in the newly fashioned outdoor classroom. All three sat down on the folding chairs. Golden introduced his lesson by saying, "Welcome to the land of the condor, named after the pair of birds you see drifting past, overhead. This morning's lessons deal with a very precious substance – gold. Through the centuries, humans have prized this metal for its beautiful luster, its durability and its comparative ease in shaping into prized objects of art.

"Many centuries ago, in South America, gold was extremely plentiful," said Golden; "please observe." Then, he activated the holovision machine. The stage lit up with a miniature Lake Guatavitá. Satch observed the mountain ring surrounding the lake. A group of people approached the lake from the background. They sang joyous songs in an unknown tongue.

As they approached, Satch noticed a group of men leading the parade. They carried a man riding on a splendidly designed chair covered by silk brocade. Even more spectacularly, he was clothed in narrow plates of gold, which flashed in the sunlight. His head was adorned with an intricate golden crown and golden rings pierced his ears.

At the lakeshore, the procession halted, but the singing continued with increased energy and verve. Then, the king-like leader stepped down from his rich throne and performed a surprising act.

He removed his golden finery, even the earrings, and began painting his body with a thick paint. Then he rolled over on the ground in a layer of gold dust until covered from head to toe in a gleaming coat.

He rose, slowly, and walked to the lakeshore, while hundreds of his followers celebrated by increasing the tempo and volume of their joyous song.

The king and several attendants entered a canoe and paddled to the middle of the lake. After lowering an anchor, the king rose and hurled golden and emerald objects into the depths. Upon finishing, the gilded man leaped from the boat. A flash of brightness and then a large splash sent his followers into a mighty cheer. Soon, the king returned to shore, and set off a festival of song and dance.

Golden flipped the holovision switch. To detect his reaction, he and Immortality studied Satch. The Sasquatch's eyes had opened wider at such rich sights.

"How can they throw away gold, like that?" asked the bewildered Satch.

Golden and Immortality chuckled together as if sharing a private joke. Then Golden turned to his curious pupil and replied, "I'm pleased that you asked about that. It's true that the tribe's kings performed this ritual once each year for centuries. A huge amount of gold had settled to the bottom of that lake. But, you see, gold was not always prized for its monetary value. Often, its only value was in its decorative capability. The people you saw throwing away their gold didn't use it as cash. They used coffee beans for that.

"The yearly ceremony which you observed was performed because of a desire for spiritual purification – a sort of cleansing and beginning over with a fresh start. This was rather like humans making their New Year's resolutions. The golden ritual symbolized a desire to remove outward appearances and become partners again with nature."

"Well, I'm sure glad they weren't throwing away money," said Satch." I don't think it's right to waste what you've earned." The Satquatch paused a moment and then asked, "But gold is money for most people, so haven't others tried to mine the lake?"

Golden smiled and answered, "Yes, there have been many who have lost their lives in pursuit of this wealth. In their greed, Europeans have trekked throughout South America in the gold chase. Often, they fail. But sometimes they've succeeded in enriching themselves at the expense of their fellow man. Let's view the next scene."

In a wink, the classroom lit up with perfect three-dimensional forms. A bearded white man in an elaborate quilted and metal uniform led a marching group of soldiers onto a dirt road outside a town lined with adobe huts. After a short, dusty march, the white invaders were met by an Indian carried on a litter, so decorated with jewelry that it seemed to emit a continual riot of colorful sparks.

The captain of the white soldiers spoke to the Indian leader in Spanish (translated into English for Satch's benefit), "I am Captain-general Francisco Pizzaro. The queen of Spain has named me governor of Peru. I demand that you and your people become Christians."

With that stiff introduction, Pizarro's chaplain handed the Indian ruler a Bible. The Indian hurled the book to the dusty street in disgust, replying angrily, "I am the king and living god, Atahualpa. My people have no need for your false religion."

Pizarro signaled his men to open fire with their muskets. In the uproar, Atahualpa was taken prisoner by the Spanish soldiers.

The scene shifted to a large prison cell, where Atahualpa was being interrogated by Pizarro's men.

"Where is your gold?" demanded one.

"It is spread throughout my kingdom," answered the king.

The soldier pressed, "How much is it worth?"

Atahualpa answered, "It is priceless." Then he added, "If you will release me, I will fill this cell with gold as high as I can reach."

This offer astounded the king's captors. They looked at each other with startled eyes and gaping mouths. The cell was huge – about 17 by 25 feet.

Following a lengthy discussion with Pizarro, the soldiers told Atahualpa, "Fine. We figure that amount of gold is worth about $15,000,000. Just get it here within two months, and you'll be released."

Quickly, llama loads of gold poured in from all over Peru. Palaces and temples were stripped of their ornaments and utensils of gold. The distances were great, and it took nearly two months to fill the cell. Just before the deadline, the ransom was complete.

Still, the Spaniards held Atahualpa captive, refusing to live up to their end of the deal. Finally, some of Pizarro's men decided to bring the Indian ruler to trial on ridiculous charges of idol worship, having more than one wife, the murder of his half-brother and treason against Spain. Swiftly, the king was sentenced to death.

Golden switched off the holovision set. Satch sat shaking his head in disbelief. After awhile, he muttered, "That poor king. He was murdered for gold – and for someone else's greed."

"Exactly!" nodded Golden in agreement. "That has been one of our biggest problems with mankind. Throughout history, they have slaughtered one another to enrich themselves. Rather than the exception, that has been the rule. It's sad."

Satch pondered his teacher's words a moment and then said, "I saw it at work when I played basketball. Some players would resort to almost any means of beating us when they saw that our team might win the championship cash. Now I understand. It's all part of an instinct in humans to claw their way to the top."

"Well said, Earthling. You understand the problem. Now, this next scene will prove that the problem didn't always exist."

The classroom stage flashed to life. The scene centered on the outside of an Indian hut. The holovision lens zoomed in, and entered the hut. The interior resembled a palace of a king. Shining golden ornaments, figurines and vessels filled the simple mud-brick walls.

An old leather-faced Indian with long straight hair adjusted his only piece of clothing, a loincloth, and exited through the open front of the hut. Outside a passersby could view the priceless treasures inside. Surprisingly, no one entered the hut to steal the gleaming golden treasures, even though the owner was gone. They just kept on strolling by, disregarding the wealth inside.

The stage darkened and Golden said, "Well, Earthling, you've seen it, but I can tell from your look of disbelief, as well as your thoughts, that you don't believe it."

Satch nodded, "Yes, sir, Mr. Golden, it is very hard to believe. I just figured that men stole from each other whenever they had a chance. Please explain."

With a broad grin, Golden replied, "We taught Earthlings the ancient art of making gold…"

"But that's crazy," interrupted Satch, "everyone knows that gold is mined – not made!"

"All that proves," said Golden, "is that Earthlings have forgotten the important procedure which we taught them. Some of your early scientists, the alchemists, spent their lives searching to relearn the secret process. A few even succeeded. But, long before, when our instructions were fresh in people's minds, there existed a truly Golden Age. Everyone owned as much gold as they pleased. That's why there was no need to steal. Observe."

The yellow teacher activated the teaching machine. A cluttered workshop-laboratory appeared on the stage. Four men busied themselves in various ways. An old grizzled man in a long robe sat on a low stool pumping a bellows to fan an open fireplace. A large earthenware pot with a glass-domed lid sizzled amid glowing embers. A long spout angled downward from the dome to a smaller collecting bowl. A youthful assistant sat observing his master's work. Near the rear of the room, two other men sat at a crude stone table mixing unknown powders with mortars and pestles. From the ceiling a single moth-eaten fish hung suspended from a rope.

Yet another fireplace smoldered in the rear. Other earthen pots and glassware steamed from the heat. The entire room seemed enclosed by shelves of important looking containers of various shapes. Beside the front fireplace, a large yellow-paged book was propped up against some metal pokers and tongs.

The ancient master spoke in a strange language (again translated for Satch's benefit) to his young helpmate, "You must memorize these steps, my son, for I am old and the process must be maintained even after I am gone. This has been ordered by our original masters, from whom all wisdom derived.

"You must remember the two vital processes, namely, constructing the philosopher's stone, and then how to use it in changing common lead into gold. Begin with a clump of orchicalcum, obtained in abundance from Atlantis. Reduce it through distillation to its basic parts. You will know when you have succeeded, for the entire room will be filled with a most wonderful sweet smell.

"This gas must be sent through glass coils, cooled and returned to a liquid state. This liquid must be carefully stored in a vial, with stopper, away from heat, since it is highly explosive. Such liquid is called mercurical water and it will evaporate almost immediately if left open.

"Next, mercurical water must be added to salts of gold which have been washed in distilled water several times. A slight hissing sound tells you that…"

Satch heard no more of the mysterious recipe for making gold. As the old man droned on, Satch nodded slightly and dozed off. He jerked to attention several minutes later as the voice said, "The heat is gradually raised and from white the color changes to citrine and finally to red – the Philosopher's Stone!"

Satch shouted, "Yay; way to go!"

Golden eyed Satch, sternly, and said, "Hush! Don't interrupt. Next comes the exciting part."

The old man leaned over, picked up an earthen jar and then sat upright again. He tipped the jar on its side and a rough ball of Philosopher's Stone rolled out into his hand. After returning the jar to the floor, he picked up a small knife and began scraping the red substance into a pot, well heated from the flames.

"Add a few scrapings to the pot of melted lead, together with a small sprinkle of gold filings like these, and watch," said the old man. As soon as he dropped the small bits of gold filings into the mixture, a thick cloud of smoke plumed upward, accompanied by a sharp crackling noise.

Moments later, the old man beamed and shouted, "It is done!" He removed the pot from the fire with metal tongs and, as if by magic, the lead had changed to gold.

Satch stared, intently, fully recovered from his earlier drowsiness. The scene dimmed.

The Rainbow teacher said, "So now you understand the secret of the Golden Age. You could even make some gold, yourself, if you could obtain some orchicalcum. But the only source of this mineral lies in Atlantis at the bottom of the sea. You'd have a difficult time finding it."

Satch said, "Well, that's OK. I didn't really want to make gold anyhow." He didn't mention that he'd dozed off during part of the process and missed some important steps. No need to upset his teacher, he guessed.

"I've enjoyed teaching you, Earthling," said Golden, with a friendly smile. "Now, my task is finished. You deserve a lunch break. This afternoon, Immortality will instruct you."

As if hearing himself beckoned, Immortality approached them from the direction of the spacecraft. Satch hadn't even noticed that he'd been absent from part of the lesson. The chocolate brown teacher carried a pan in front of his chest. As he approached the pair, he said, "Here is a treat you should enjoy – direct from our Rainbow Galley. Earthlings call it 'Surprise Peach Kuchen' – a delightful cake topped with a glaze of peach slices, sugar and cinnamon. It serves 10 – 12 people, so that should satisfy you."

Satch beamed and nearly inhaled the whole cake through

his nose. He reached out and accepted the food. "Thanks a lot!" he said, flashing appreciative gazes at both of his teachers. "But first, recess," he told the startled pair. Without further explanation, he removed his clothes, raced the short distance to the edge and plunged into the cool lake. Nearly a minute later, he emerged, sputtering and splashing near the center of the lake. Satch felt a welcome relief from the blazing sunlight which had baked him all morning long.

At last, he swam gracefully back to shore, flopped down beside the cake and stuffed it down in five huge gulps. Golden and Immortality stood quietly, nearby, observing the Sasquatch's strange feeding traits.

Satch reclined on his back, pressing the sand with his shoulder blades and shifted sideways several times to build a nest-like hole. Then he dozed off.

VIII

Immortality's Lesson

Nearly an hour later, Satch awoke to the coaxing of Immortality. The brown Rainbow teacher seemed impatient as he said, firmly, "You must get up and return to class. I have deadlines to meet."

Satch squinted, drowsily, and muttered, "Oh, no. More classes? When does it end?"

"This afternoon is your last class on Earth."

Satch winced at the shocking answer and almost choked on his next question, "Do you mean I'm going to die?"

Immortality's face brightened, momentarily, and he smiled, reassuringly, saying, "Oh, no! I mean not now. You misunderstood me. I meant to say that tomorrow we're leaving Earth for a while. But don't be alarmed. We promised to return you safely to your home on Earth. Returning to your question on death, it's true that you and other Earthlings are destined to experience death, each in your own due time."

Satch weighed his teacher's words several moments. His eyes misted over with sadness. "Yes, I know," said Satch, solemnly, "but I don't like to think about it."

"Cheer up!" ordered Immortality. Then he added, "It's not as bad as all that. Surely you can tell from my name that death is not the end."

"Really?" asked Satch, warming a bit to his teacher. "Why not?"

Immortality eyed his pupil, evenly, and continued, "Well, first you must understand that your body is composed of atoms which, even after physical death, continue their individual existence. So while it's true that your temporary physical form is discontinued, your permanent form at the atomic level continues on."

Satch said, "Yes, but my temporary form is me, while my separate atoms won't be me at all. Won't I cease to exist?"

"Not at all. You see, your separate atoms contain memory imprints of your total existence. Some Earthlings have called this memory the Soul. Whatever its name, your substance and meaning actually multiplies billions of times upon physical death. In effect, your entity becomes billions of separate imprints of the original. In short, physical death becomes the ultimate reproduction of yourself."

"But," persisted Satch, "I won't be able to run and exercise when I'm dead. So what fun is that?"

"Imagine the memory of those enjoyable times repeated, endlessly, in billions of separate places," said Immortality. "Then I think you can see why I speak joyfully of death. Earthlings naturally fear the unknown elements of death. But, in most cases, the fear of dying is overblown."

Satch pondered his teacher's words a moment, grinned happily and shouted, "I've got it! I've got it! That's Heaven – the multiplied memory of your own life! Well, I'll be a silly Sasquatch!"

Immortality beamed and said, "Well stated, Earthling. Your understanding has reached…"

"And the opposite," interrupted Satch, "the opposite is, you know – I hate to say it, but anyway, here goes – Hell – if you lead a bad life, then afterwards… afterwards, the misery becomes magnified agony. Well, now I've got it! I feel so great! I understand! Wow!"

Immortality strained to keep his composure, but his pleasure increased, noticeably. His face filled with a warm, toothy smile which spread nearly from ear to ear. He started nodding and repeating, "Go on...go on...go on." Then he stiffened and forced the sheer joy from his face. Forcing a serious look, Immortality continued his skillful teaching by saying, "I suppose you're wondering why the Rainbow Race seems to live forever. But your stay on Earth, as a single living creature, is so short. After all, we mentioned, shortly after we contacted you, that we were billions of years old. Do you wonder?"

"Yes, of course, I wonder," said Satch, still aglow from his recent mind storms. "How can you live for billions of years?"

The brown teacher turned more serious, nearly sorrowful, and answered, "We are not actually alive. Therefore, we have no souls. We are ultimate machines, robots, automatons, or whatever you choose to call us. We were created by human-like beings on a distant planet.

"They created us out of machinery and laboratory-cultured cellular material. So, while our outer wrappers appear living, many limitations are created by our machine cores. For example, our thinking is limited to pre-determined programs built into us by our creators. The joy you saw on my face, minutes ago, could not last. In fact, I was shaken by its occurrence. You see, I was designed to exist as a joyless worker – in effect, my master's sorrowful slave. I have struggled, literally fought, to obtain some degree of normal emotions. Now, at last, I can force myself into temporary joy."

Satch eyed his teacher, mournfully, and said, "That's really too bad. I find joy in many ways – eating peaches, running, sleeping under my pine forest sky and just being wild. I love to live!"

"So, too, would I love to live," said Immortality, gloomily, "but my living has been severely curtailed. It's the same with the rest. For example, Strength, as his name implies, possesses awesome physical ability for his size, but he cannot master gentleness, no matter how hard he tries. Consequently, we must keep him away from our advanced gadgets, lest he tear off a lever or punch a button completely into the device. Oh, he tries to ease up, but his programming prevents it.

"Each Rainbow being exists with definite limitations not built into other entities. Your only limitation is lack of knowledge, and that may be obtained if you seek it out. Knowledge, then, becomes your tool to experience the entire range of living emotions: joy, sadness, pride, compassion, love, hate and fear. In sum, you may really live, while we, as machines, may only exist.

"Another thing, even though we've been around for so long, ours is a constant struggle with recharging energy packs, replacing worn parts, and perhaps, worst of all, we have no souls. Should we meet destruction, that's it. Nothingness. Halt. That's why our struggle for lengthy existence becomes so important to us."

Satch pondered Immortality's words, momentarily, and then quipped, "So there are more teaching machines around than the holovision projectors! You're one!"

Immortality nodded, sadly, and then replied, "That's right – Rainbow Race teaching machines."

"But, why can't we have it both ways?" asked Satch, pressing his teacher for further insight. "Your lengthy existence and our wide range of life emotions? That seems like a perfect solution."

Immortality said, "We're way ahead of you. That's already been done. In fact, there are humans walking around on Earth, today, who have lived for thousands of years. You could not tell them from your friends, the Stevensons. But, you see, they no longer have blood, organs and bones. And they are subject to all of the rigorous maintenance care I told you about, before. We could fix you up like that, if you wish."

Immortality's words rocked Satch's eardrums, and he turned several shades paler at the thought. "N – No," he stammered. "Don't get any ideas about turning my body into a machine. I …I like it just fine as it is."

"Well," said Immortality, "I just wanted you to know that the opportunity is there. What you choose is your own business."

The relieved Sasquatch regained his color and said, "Wow! Can I change the subject? I've been wanting to know more about that spacecraft. It moves around in the neatest ways – darting this way and that, seemingly ignoring gravity. How about that?"

Immortality nodded and answered, "Yes, indeed. For the remaining lessons, I must turn you over to Courage. He's our spacecraft captain, and I know that he intends to share this information with you. But, first, we'll need to climb aboard the spacecraft and get some rest. I can tell that you're exhausted. Come."

Immortality motioned Satch to follow, and the pair began their short hike back to the gleaming craft. Before entering, Satch paused at the top of the ramp and bid silent farewell to the gold-filled lake high in the Columbian mountains.

IX

The

Space Ark

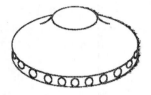

At dawn the next morning, Satch woke to the soft continuous hum of the spacecraft engines. As he blinked the sleep from his eyes, he noted the muted outlines of empty bunks. He felt the separation between the two small bunks set end-to-end beneath his husky frame.

"Earthling," came a voice from an unseen source, "please report to the flight control cabin at your earliest chance."

Satch looked around the bunk cabin for the speaker and spotted a small box on one wall, which, upon closer inspection resembled an intercom. He pressed the "Talk" button and announced, "I'm on my way."

The drowsy Sasquatch made his way out of the bunkroom, down several cramped passageways, and finally spotted a sign with an arrow saying, "Flight Control." He took a sharp right turn and opened a bulky metal door. As Satch entered, several Rainbow beings saluted him and flashed fleeting smiles. Others of his tiny colored instructors busied themselves with the controls. They seemed all present, but Satch didn't bother to count bodies.

"Good morning," said Courage, the red one. He extended his right arm in a salute. Then he and Satch shook hands. Courage said, "If we appear happy, today, it is because we're going home."

Satch beamed at the news, but then caught himself up short with uncertainty. He asked, cautiously, "Am I going home, today?"

"Yes, of course," said Courage. "But, first, we must visit our Rainbow home – near Venus. Your lessons must include our most important field trip – an inspection of the Space Ark. As we mentioned in our discussions, Earth astronomers have spotted the Ark near Venus. Naturally, they assumed that our home was a moon circling the planet. When we found out we'd been discovered, we moved over to the planet's hidden side. Ever since then, your scientists have wondered what became of Venus' moon."

Satch looked puzzled and asked, "But why did you try to hide the truth from our astronomers?"

Courage's eyes flashed approval at Satch's inquiring mind. "Excellent! Excellent!" he said. "I can see that you are attempting to understand everything. It's simply this: humans instinctively fear invasion by beings from other worlds. This fear drives them to irrational behavior. During the 1930s, a radio program described an invasion by machine-like super beings from Mars. Literally thousands of persons panicked and began acting like lunatics in an attempt to escape the urban scene. This plunge toward supposed safety meant that many were killed in the crush.

"If a make-believe story can create such madness, just imagine the chaos which might occur if people met the real thing – us. But, times are changing. Humans have become more conditioned to the possibility of our existence. Movies, television and actual sightings of our spacecraft – what your Earthlings call 'flying saucers' – have combined to convince a large portion of the human population that we really do exist.

"So, now, we feel that the time is right to reveal our existence through you. We can only hope that you will be believed," concluded Courage. Then, as an afterthought, he added, "Now, please remain alert and enjoy the trip."

Moments later, Satch observed the familiar sensation of watching the Earth drop rapidly below, while feeling no sensation of movement. The Sasquatch peered through the windshield as Courage began a verbal travelogue, "Look, Earthling, observe how the land has changed. Look to your left. Notice the edge of the sea. The land looks like a mountain, while the sea has become like a canal."

The spacecraft rose still further and Courage continued, "Look, Earthling, how the Earth has changed. Now it looks like a plantation of trees."

Climbing faster, straight upward, the spacecraft flew. Courage said, "Now notice how the world has changed. The land has turned into a cake and the vast sea has become the size of a puddle of mud."

The spacecraft carried them ever faster and higher. Finally, Courage intoned, "Look down and see how the Earth has disappeared – the land, the sea, both gone, now."

Satch gulped loudly and saw that it was true. His knees quavered as his eyes searched in vain for his former home. "Stop!" he shouted, in fear. "I must return to Earth, to my home!" Huge tears squeezed their way from beneath his heavy eyelids as he realized that his home now seemed out of reach.

"Do not become alarmed," comforted Courage. "We told you that you would be returned safely to your home. You may trust our word. Now, try to relax and enjoy the trip."

"Relax!" said Satch, angrily. "That's easy for you to say. You're going home!" His knees ached from nervous tension. His eyes continued searching the total blackness for traces of the Earth he'd left behind.

"Look up above," commanded Courage, "see the constellations in all their glory. More stars than you've ever been able to see before. Millions of them! Many have planetary systems very similar to your own. Be comforted that you are not alone. There are countless other planets just like your Earth."

"But, it's the only home I've got!" wailed Satch.

"Correction," said Courage. "The only home you've known. Soon, you will know our home."

Onward, into the blackness they flew. Satch forced himself to relax, as best he could. It seemed useless to fight the experience, he thought.

After a brief time, Courage shouted, "Look! Up above! The Space Ark!"

Satch strained his eyes upward and to the left. Then he spotted a glowing, football-shaped object. Directly to its right, a bright cloud-covered globe dominated his view. "That must be Venus," said Satch.

"Right," said Strength. "Space Ark approaching on the left. Venus approaching on the right."

The distance between the spacecraft and Space Ark decreased rapidly, and soon the spacecraft began slowing down. It seemed to hover gently awhile and then began settling toward the mother ship.

Spacecraft III drifted gently up against the Space Ark, like a leaf falling, casually, to the ground. It attached itself effortlessly to an umbilical tube. Satch could see several other identical spacecrafts similarly attached along the side of the larger ship.

The loud hum of the engines stopped. The Rainbow crew busied themselves with docking procedures, silently and without pause. Satch watched, impressed by the teamwork of the crew.

At last, the space travelers lined up in formation, two by two, and began marching toward a hatch connecting the spacecraft with the umbilical tube. Courage motioned Satch to come along. As they completed passage through the tube, Satch sighed in relief because he could, at last, stand upright.

Nature opened a hatch and the triumphant crew was greeted by the blare of a Rainbow band playing the Veskin national anthem. Each crewmember received handshakes and hugs from a gathering crowd of Rainbow beings.

Satch stepped into the parent ship. A gasp rose from the crowd as they spotted the giant Sasquatch. In unison, they shrank backwards, slightly. Moments later, they relaxed a bit.

Courage raised his arm and shouted, "Fellow Rainbow beings! Listen! We have brought an Earthling here to show him our home. Please carry on your normal lives. We have promised him a safe return home. So please cooperate."

These words repelled the crowd. They turned, spread out and resumed their daily tasks. Satch noted a huge hangar area ahead of him where several spacecraft rested among various pieces of repair machines.

"The spacecraft garage," said Strength, motioning toward the activity.

At the far end of the hangar, the group climbed a short stairway and entered a smaller room filled with troughs of green, scummy material. "Our oxygen delivery room," announced Nature, proudly. "Each trough provides chemicals, which stimulate algae growth. The algae provide oxygen as a waste product, which is piped into all sections of the Space Ark. This system allows us to breathe."

Moving through the second floor, the group entered a huge room, which resembled a greenhouse. Beads of sweat popped out on Satch's forehead as the group inspected each blossom and vegetable stalk. Satch noticed that many of the plants appeared larger than similar Earth types and were literally overcoming some of the smaller plants. "Great fruits and vegetables, here," he thought, feeling a drop of drool form at the corner of his mouth.

"This area provides all of our food," said Strength. "We

grow fruit and vegetables, but without the use of soil. Our plants are grown by hydroponics – using liquid chemicals, alone."

Exiting through a door at the far end, Satch and the Rainbow teachers entered the Space Ark's flight control room. It contained instruments similar to those on the spacecraft only the room was much larger and more complex. Rows of gleaming panels, dials, gauges, levers, switches and foot pedals lined the wall directly in front of the massive windshield. The group paused and then walked through another doorway.

They walked up a flight of stairs, through another doorway and Satch's eyes widened at the sight of an enormous recreation room. Dozens of Rainbow beings busied themselves with lifting weights. Others played pinball machines, billiards, swimming, wrestling and ping-pong.

Some of the activities contained elements of levitation: ping-pong balls bounded back, guided only by the players' thoughts, without paddles; billiard balls careened around the tables without being struck by cue sticks; and no one bothered to touch the pinball machines, which flashed and rang crazily, controlling them with their minds. A player thought the ball up the chute and made it travel toward the choicest spots for accumulating the most points.

Satch approached a billiard table and stared in amazement with open mouth. "I sure wish I could do that," he said, openly admiring the ability to create action with thought, alone. Then, catching himself, he quickly retreated, saying, "Well, I do and I don't. That would require an operation on my brain. So, no, I think I'll keep on playing those games the old fashioned way."

"As you wish, Earthling," said Golden, politely.

Then Courage motioned the group forward into the next room. The red leader paused beside the door, saying, "This is Rainbow Village, where we live.

A gleaming, sparkling sight dazzled Satch. The room,

several times higher than any of the others, resembled a
diamond-studded crown. Thousands of hexagonal panels were
arranged in staggered layers, forming small apartment cubicles.
Each door was painted a different color – a greater variety of
colors than Satch could imagine even in his wildest dreams.

"You see," said Flesh, the pink teacher, "every Rainbow
being has been created a different color and each door matches
his own special tint. In fact, color represents our only true
identifying trait. Naturally, each of us takes great pride in our
own unique hue. Similarly, the names of most humans make
them proud."

They moved onward through another doorway and into a
richly carpeted room, decorated entirely in red. It was shaped
somewhat like a bowl. At the bottom, a long hardwood table
surrounded by 24 chairs rested in the center of the room's only
flat area. Steps radiated upward like starfish arms, leading to
tiers of viewing benches surrounding the central arena.

"The Council Room," said the violet teacher, Woe. "Each
of your instructors served on the Rainbow Council, together
with a dozen others. In this room, we planned your education,
along with other major decisions mentioned before."

Satch's mind flashed back to some of the major decisions:
the extermination of the giant reptiles, the creation of humans,
the great flood, the destruction of Atlantis – and he felt deeply
awed by his important place in history.

"We'll meet here, shortly, to discuss your final instructions
before returning to Earth," said Nature, "but, first, I'd like you to
inspect our Rainbow Zoo."

Nature led the group up a flight of carpeted stairs and
through an arched entryway. Several corridors later, they
stopped at a small door. Nature opened it, and Satch felt a burst
of warm, dry air. Intense artificial sunlight bathed the desert
scene, below. A cactus forest, a few in bloom, harbored a rich

variety of desert animals: various types of lizards, snakes, insects and birds. A few scurried about, but most sought shelter in and around the cacti, avoiding the midday heat.

The group visited several other artificial habitats, which comprised the Rainbow Zoo. Satch was keenly interested in the jungle habitat, especially when he noticed the multitude of primates: monkeys, orangutans, chimpanzees, gorillas and apes. He actually rushed up and hugged a pair of Sasquatches, which had been drinking at the water hole. Even though the animals could not speak to Satch, they beamed and trumpeted friendly recognition, "Eee - ooo -- wah! Eee - ooo - wah!" The Rainbow teachers nodded approval and traces of smiles creased several of their faces.

It seemed as if Satch intended to take up permanent residence in the jungle. Finally, he was coaxed back to the waiting group. They returned to the Rainbow Council Room. At the long table Courage motioned Satch to take a seat at the end. The others sat down on both sides near Satch.

"Now, it is time for the debriefing session," said Courage. It is always best to review one's lessons. Also, we need to instruct you on how to spread the news when you return to Earth."

Satch nodded, signaling that he was alert.

Courage began, "First, never forget the destruction of Veskin by the Trobelites, nor our escape in the Space Ark toward your sun. Also recall the formation of your solar system and the destruction of the sixth planet."

"Also," added Nature, "recall the beginnings of plant and animal life on Earth."

"Of course," said Flesh, "our experiments in creating human beings from their Sasquatch and Rainbow parents are extremely important to recall. Further, increasing mind power through trepanning must be recalled. Be kind to plants, because they have feelings, too. Also, remember the levitation exercises and eidetic memory."

Next, Strength added, "Earthling, recall the implantation of lasers in humans, which enabled them to cut huge blocks of stone for building massive structures, such as pyramids."

Woe continued, "Don't forget the tremendous flood we caused, and the safety of the chosen humans within the Great Pyramid."

"Nor should you forget what we did to the island content of Atlantis," boasted Torrent.

"I hope you will reserve a special place in your memory for the Philosopher's Stone and the gold-makers," Golden said.

"And remember about dying," said Immortality. "Earthlings should not fear death because they have a soul which continues to live."

When the teachers had finished reviewing, their star pupil said, "How could I forget any of this? It was all so real that I feel like I actually lived these events. And the holovision…when will that become available to humans? That is incredible!"

"Well," said Strength, "the big thing, now, on Earth, is 'High Definition' television. HDTV is currently in its infancy. As that medium becomes more and more real, the next step will be Holovision – but that's years away."

"OK", said Satch, "but what now? You said that you wanted me to spread the word to humans. But how?"

Carefully, Courage responded to Satch's questions, "We made certain that you missed your supermarket engagement so that many people would wonder about your absence. Also, to prove your visit to the area of Venus, we would like to give you this stone." Courage handed Satch an ordinary-looking rock.

"Your scientists," he continued, "should be able to note that it is different from any Earth stone. As we mentioned at the outset, your reputation has been superb. We believe that humans admire and respect you and will, therefore, believe you. Call a news conference when you return. Show the reporters your Venus stone, the circular mark left in the field from our exhaust and, simply, tell the truth. How could they disbelieve you?"

Satch digested these instructions a moment and then answered, "Well, maybe you're right. I'll do as you say. But what if …"

"…they still don't believe you?" Courage completed Satch's thoughts. "Well, then, in that case we'll probably have to take further steps."

"Further steps?" said the puzzled Satch.

Courage replied, "Yes. Perhaps further action to eradicate human life. You see, we feel that we have been patient in the extreme. Ultimately, we plan to move the Rainbow Race to Earth. But in its present condition: warring nations, greed, violence, pollution and terrorism – we know that the planet is quickly becoming a wasteland. Unless humans can solve these problems, soon, then we'll be forced to take further steps. So, you see, your message must include thoughts like cooperation, good will, peace and interdependency. Humans must understand that what happens to one, happens to all – either bad or good. It's their choice. Will they listen? I'd say they must."

Courage's words echoed and re-echoed in Satch's head until he felt a splitting headache overcome him. He slumped in his chair and a glassy stare nestled itself between his hairy eyebrows and cheekbones.

The Rainbow teachers sat, silently, for several minutes gazing toward the tormented Satch. Then, as if on some invisible signal, they rose in unison and motioned to Satch to follow them. Single file, with Satch in the rear, they climbed a stairway to the top of the Council Room. Several rights and lefts down corridors brought them to a glass hallway. Satch gulped as he gazed downward into the empty blackness of space. He noted the spaceships attached to their tubular umbilical cords. At the third one, the group descended a circular stairway, entered the tube, and, moments later, secured themselves within Spacecraft III.

Satch's headache overcame him completely, and he stretched out full length on the carpeted floor of Control Central. Thus stupefied, he blocked out the hum, the changing lights and the half hour flight back to Earth.

X

The

Homecoming

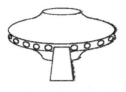

"Earthling, get up!"

Satch blinked a moment and then saw that a red face stood over him staring downward.

"Guess where we are," ordered Courage.

Satch said, "Home, I hope." Nervous tension had caused every muscle in his body to ache.

Courage smiled broadly and chirped, "Right! We have landed in the exact spot in your field where we met you three days ago."

Satch bolted to his feet and rushed over to the windshield. It was true. To his left, gently illuminated by moonlight, stood the dark outline of the Stevenson home. To his right, he noted his own friendly pine forest canopy.

"Please let me go," begged Satch.

Courage said, "Not so fast. I nearly forgot one of our most important lessons. So, school's not dismissed, yet."

"Oh, no," said Satch. "What now?"

"The spacecraft, itself. We want you to understand a bit of how it works. I won't go into too much detail, as I know you're eager to get home. Basically, the craft operates with two energy types. All of our electrical needs are provided through a plutonium reactor near the bottom of the craft. The exhaust is emitted through hundreds of tiny openings in the base. That's why the grass beneath us right now is seared.

"But, most importantly, we move about by capturing and focusing gravity rays. You see, giant double star systems, as they revolve around each other, send off huge amounts of invisible gravity rays. These are captured by any object large enough to possess a strong magnetic field. Due to their atomic structure, all objects have magnetic fields. But only huge objects, such as planets or stars, have sufficiently strong magnetic fields to attract gravity rays.

"Our secret is simple. Almost the entire outer shell of a space shuttle is composed of steel bands, which have been wound tightly with copper wires. The ends of the wires are attached to plutonium-powered batteries. In brief, the entire craft becomes a tremendously powerful electromagnet – one that attracts and captures abundant gravity rays.

"These gravity rays are collected in a device called a Gravitron Reservoir. When needed, the rays are released into the bowl-shaped Gravitron Deflector. This deflector is located directly in the shuttle's center and hundreds of tubes radiate outward from it in all directions. They lead to the outside.

"In order to deflect gravitrons, it is only necessary to reverse the electromagnetic poles. The concentrated gravitrons move with the speed of light to a point 200 feet in any direction from the craft, which begins moving toward the concentrated gravitron spot. Further series of gravitron releases keep the craft in motion, able to change directions instantly, depending on the direction and size of gravitron deposits.

"Since the craft is constantly under the control of gravity, there are no undesirable effects of inertia. For example, when you travel rapidly upward in an Earth elevator, you feel distress in your stomach, as if you were leaving it down below. Or when an automobile turns a corner suddenly, your body tends to move in a straight line, so you are thrown toward the side of the car. Such unpleasant sensations occur because the vehicles are working against gravity.

"With our system, none of that discomfort happens, since our artificial gravity always controls the craft's moves. So we can move at high speed and completely reverse our direction without feeling a thing.

"You have listened attentively, and I'm sorry to keep you so long. But this subject continually puzzles Earthlings. And so we thought the facts should be revealed. Now you may leave. Do you have your Venus rock?"

Satch held up his fist and opened it to reveal the rock to his teacher. The Sasquatch felt extreme joy at arriving home. "Good-by," he said with misty eyes. Then he dashed down the ramp and didn't stop running until he reached the first pine tree. There, he pulled up, turned and waved as the spacecraft lifted out of the field.

Quickly, Satch flopped himself down inside the most comfortable bed in the world – his rough pine bough lean-to. He barely had time to savor its prickly scratchiness before dropping into the nothingness of sleep.

During the early morning, Satch awoke to the steady "pat-pat-pat" of raindrops above his head. Most of the water rolled on down the outside, but every so often a few persistent drips squeezed through the layered greenery and dropped onto Satch's face. One stuck on his facial hair, just above his upper lip. Still half asleep, he analyzed the drop's pine scent and grinned. "That's a Washington raindrop," he thought. "That's so great!"

As if to experience the downpour, totally, Satch pulled out of his shelter, trotted along the edge of the forest for a few hundred yards and then raised his arms to the sky. He felt his entire body tingle as thousands of tiny water daggers thoroughly invigorated his mind.

He raced off in the direction of the Stevenson home. Part way across the field, he paused, momentarily to inspect the exhaust ring. It was burned even blacker than when he'd first noticed it. Now he understood why.

Continuing his excited race, Satch felt so wonderful to be free. In no time at all, his feet sloshed into some muddy ground surrounding the Stevenson's trees. Even mud squishing up between his toes felt wonderful, just then.

Almost before his 18-inch feet hit the back porch, he pounded the screen door, loudly, and yelled, "Marcie, I'm back!"

A minute later, Marcie opened the door. She stood there staring, dressed in levis and pajama top, mouth agape.

"Could I have some towels?" asked Satch, inspecting his wet and muddy body, sheepishly.

"Satch!" shouted Marcie at her missing friend. "Where have you been? You missed your supermarket date. I organized search parties and we combed every inch of woods for the past three days. I feared the worst – that you'd been kidnapped, or even murdered. It's just … just great to see you."

Ellie joined them at the kitchen door. She rounded up several towels from another part of the house and handed them to Satch. He scrubbed himself dry, paying careful attention to his muddy feet. Then he entered the kitchen with a big smile.

Quickly, his face took on a serious look. "Marcie," said Satch, "I hope you believe the story about what happened to me."

"I'm dying to hear it," answered Marcie, "but, first, let's 'do' breakfast." She motioned Satch to sit down at the kitchen table. Ellie prepared some bacon and eggs, and Satch wolfed it down. The food felt exquisite to Satch's stomach because he hadn't eaten since the Bogotá Plateau.

Afterwards, Satch related his entire story to Marcie and Ellie. They listened silently and thoughtfully. When Satch finished, Marcie rubbed her chin, as if petting a cat. "I see,

Satch. That's quite a fantastic story. For some reason, I'm still not convinced. Can you show us any evidence?"

"Oh, sure. There's the exhaust ring out in the field …and the Venus rock. Oh, my gosh! The rock! Where is it? I'm sure I had it in my hand when I left the spacecraft. Bur, I was so tired. I don't remember where I put it. Maybe it's near my shelter. Or in the field …the field … if it's there, it may be impossible to find. The field is filled with rocks. And this one is so ordinary looking. Oh, no!" wailed Satch, breaking into tears.

"Take it easy Satch," said Marcie. "You're home again and that's really the only important thing."

"But, you don't understand … people must change, or … or there will be another catastrophe and we'll all be killed!"

"Satch, that sounds like a mighty big order. I mean, really... you expect people to change their ways because of your story. Well..."

"Listen, both of you Stevensons, I can sense that you don't believe me," said Satch. "At least call a news conference for me, will you? I'm under instructions to tell my story to the news media. I'll meet with them in the field tomorrow morning.

With an optimistic look, Marcie answered, "OK, Satch. Listen, I hope our agreement still stands. You will make promotional appearances for us, won't you?"

"Uh, oh, sure, Marcie … after this business is over."

"Great. I think we can help each other."

"Right." Satch rose and told the Stevensons good-by.

The rest of that damp day, Satch searched the entire area for the Venus rock. His shelter came apart, piece-by-piece, and he tramped the area between his home and the exhaust ring over and over. It was no use. "Lost it for sure," he thought. Hundreds of thousands of rocks were strewn around his immediate vicinity. Not one of these could be identified, with certainty, as the Venus rock. At dusk, he abandoned the search and flopped into bed, completely drained.

XI

The

Air Force

Satch heard absolutely nothing for a full 12 hours. Then, at 6:00 a.m., the forest came alive with bird talk, high in the pine trees. He rose, gathered some edible plant roots and savored a familiar Northwest meal. After resting a full hour, he began his running and exercise routine.

By mid-morning, the Sasquatch strolled over to the edge of the scorched area and sat down on the grass and weeds, deep in thought. His bent knees encased his slumped head and his arms formed a wreath around his legs and head. He thought of his experiences during the past few days.

His thoughts were interrupted by a commotion in the driveway next to the Stevenson house. He looked up and spotted a caravan of jeeps heading his way across the field. "I wonder if these people are from the news media," he thought. If so, they had a strange way of arriving. Satch had expected private cars carrying reporters. Instead several dozen uniformed men in blue charged toward him.

As the leader arrived, Satch saw that he had lots of gold trim on his flat shoulder bars and more of the "scrambled eggs" on the brim of his hat. Stiffly, the officer said, "I am Major General Huggins, Special U.F.O. Investigator for the U.S. Air Force. Your name, please."

"Satch Stevenson," he replied.

"I understand you witnessed a U.F.O. sighting. If so, I will require answers to a series of questions," said Huggins.

"I requested a news conference, not an interrogation by the military," Satch shot back.

"Well, our friends in the news media always cooperate with us. You see, we always investigate sightings first, before releasing information to the public. Sometimes, we need to cordon off the area for the safety of all. What's this burned area over here?" asked the Major General, turning away from Satch.

Satch tried to tell the officer his story, but was interrupted with a sharp command, "Get that circular area roped off!"

Instantly, several other uniformed men sprang into action with posts, sledgehammers and thick ropes. Within 15 minutes, they completed their task of enclosing the circular burn. Several others walked around the perimeter carrying boxlike machines, holding them close to the ground. Then one, evidently the leader declared, "Radioactive!" He motioned toward other machines parked in the Stevenson driveway.

As Satch watched, helplessly, a bulldozer entered the field, crossed it and began chewing up the scorched area, turning over the soil. Soon, the blackened evidence was completely gone.

"Now," said Huggins, "the work is completed, and there's no danger of human contamination."

"And there's no evidence, either," said the dejected Sasquatch.

"What?" asked the Major General.

"The Venus Stone is gone. Now the exhaust ring is gone. All I have left is my story."

Huggins smiled and said, "All right. Tell us your story. Almost all of them have been answered in terms of swamp gas, ball lightning, weather balloons, meteors, comets, phases of Venus or hallucinations. No doubt, your story will fall into one of those categories. But I will keep an open mind. Go ahead."

Satch gritted his teeth and shot back, "No dice! I'm telling my story to the reporters. Since you've performed your handicraft with the bulldozer, my story is all I have left."

Huggins scowled and said, reluctantly, "As you wish. But it will be necessary to leave several guards here for awhile to see that nobody enters the danger zone."

Satch perceived that every word – every action – by the Air Force was calculated to cover up the facts. He grew angrier by the moment, teeth clenched and face turning red. "GET OUT OF HERE!" Satch bellowed the words like shots from a machine gun.

Huggins jerked away. Part of the uniformed group turned and walked back toward their jeeps, while a few others hoisted rifles to their shoulders and began patrolling the cordoned zone. Satch sat down, solemnly, on the stubble field and waited for reporters to arrive.

He didn't have to wait long. The news media began arriving shortly after Huggins and the jeeps exited the Stevenson driveway. Satch could see that the Major General paused several minutes as reporters surrounded him.

Afterwards, their cars hurried across the field toward Satch and the bulldozed "danger zone." Their rapid-fire questions caused his head to swim. Moments later, he yelled, "Stop!" His heavy voice boomed out like a cannon blast. The reporters shrank back several steps and stilled themselves.

Satch related every detail to the men and women, as they jotted down key phrases in a variety of notebooks and steno pads. Afterwards, several reporters asked pointed questions.

"May we see the Venus rock?"

"I told you I lost it."

"Oh, yes, you said you lost it."

"What about the exhaust burn?"

"It was right over there." Satch pointed at the bulldozed spot.

"I don't see anything but a plowed area that has been roped off and guarded."

"Well, the Air Force bulldozed it. Don't ask me why. Ask them. Now, I'd like you to leave me alone," the weary Satch requested. "I've been having a splitting headache, and the questioning has made it worse."

Satch turned and trudged back toward the woods.

Some of the puzzled reporters shook their heads. Others got on their cell phones. Within minutes, they had left the field in their cars.

XII

The SAINTS

The following day, Satch reviewed the press clippings at the Stevenson house. "Awful! Terrible!" he said, mournfully, as Marcie and Ellie watched Satch scan the articles. A funeral parlor gloom hung over the living room. "They don't believe me at all. Marcie, you believe me, don't you?"

"You know, I'd really like to believe you," said Marcie. "It's just that … well, it's all so fantastic. It reminds me of science fiction."

Just then, the phone rang, and Ellie hurried out to the kitchen to answer it. She returned in a moment and said, "It's for you, Satch."

Satch rose and long stepped it across the house to the phone, "Hello. Satch Stevenson speaking."

"Hello. You don't know me, but my name is Howard Spaulding. I'm an elder in an organization called the "Saucer Anti-Interference Network Team", or SAINT, for short. We are very eager to have you address our Seattle chapter."

"You want me to give a speech to your club?"

"Well, yes, we'd be very honored. We would arrange transportation, meals and lodging during your stay. Agreed?"

"Sounds fine to me," said Satch, brightening at the prospect of reaching a friendly audience.

Spaulding said, "Great! Our meeting is set for tomorrow

night. Could I pick you up at 2:00 tomorrow afternoon?"

"Sure," answered Satch. "Do you know how to get here?"

"Of course; your address was listed in every newspaper article."

"Every newspaper article?" asked Satch. "How many have you read?"

Spaulding paused a moment to reflect. Then he said, cautiously, "Oh, I suppose about 60. You see, my email in-box receives U.F.O. stories sent by other SAINT members in every major city in the United States."

"Well, tell me," said Satch, "did anybody believe me?"

"Interestingly enough, the tone of every article was either disbelief or skeptical neutrality. No, I'm afraid very few persons believe you."

"But, then, why do you want me to speak to your group?" asked the puzzled Sasquatch.

"Because … well …we're different. We strive to uncover the truth in these matters. You'll find us a responsive audience."

Satch answered, "OK, then, see you tomorrow."

"Right. See you then."

For diversion, Satch helped Marcie and her younger brother, Ralph, build a storage shed for the rest of the day and the next morning. Marcie took advantage of the Sasquatch's enormous strength to lift several massive ceiling beams into place.

Around 2:00, a shiny blue Toyota entered the long driveway beside the Stevenson house. Satch waved and approached the car. After confirming Spaulding's identity, Satch got into the car and they backed out of the driveway.

Spaulding was dressed in a conservative gray business suit with black tie and shoes. As Satch examined the driver, he felt self-conscious at his own clothing: levis and tee shirt. Satch noticed a small tie clip in the form of a rainbow, half way down Spaulding's tie. "Probably just a coincidence," thought Satch.

The Sasquatch admired the friendly fir forests, which

emerged from scrub pines as they headed west across the mountain pass.

Once in Seattle, Spaulding crossed a couple of bridges and pulled up beside an old brick building in a run-down section of the city. Satch spotted a sign above a musty doorway, which read "S.A.I.N.T."

"Here we are," said Spaulding. As Spaulding got out of the car, Satch sensed something unusual about the man's motions – something so subtle that he couldn't identify it. Satch concluded that Spaulding was just a bit different.

They entered the arched doorway and climbed a flight of stairs. The pair went through an inside door and entered a recreation area filled with pool tables. To his right, Satch noted a large auditorium. To the left, he saw a kitchen area.

"Let's have something to eat," said Spaulding. They walked into the kitchen, and two lady cooks were startled by the size of the hairy giant. One of them started to scream and, simultaneously, dropped a glass to the floor, where it shattered into a hundred pieces.

After composing themselves, the cooks served up plates heaped full with roast beef, string beans, baked potatoes and salad. Satch joined Spaulding at a nearby table. Soon, several other men with loaded plates joined the pair.

Satch didn't bother looking up until his plate was clean. Then he saw that each newcomer wore the same style of clothing: gray suits, with black ties and shoes. Upon further observation, Satch discovered that each man wore the same tiny rainbow tie clip, just like Spaulding's. In fact, the only differences Satch noted were the men's sizes and physical appearances. They even ate alike, sort of jerky, as if each muscle action were separately controlled.

Spaulding introduced Satch to the five others and told him that they comprised the SAINT Board of Elders. The group engaged in small talk while waiting for the auditorium to fill. When it became time for the meeting to begin, the Elders whisked Satch up out of his chair and hustled him up front past the darkened seating area to the raised, floodlit stage.

As the Elders and Satch sat down on a row of metal chairs, a swell of applause began, slowly, rhythmically and politely. It took Satch's eyes several minutes to adjust to the bright lights. Slowly, he saw that the entire auditorium had filled. He was not too surprised to see that the men in the audience each wore the same gray and black clothes. He'd begun expecting that. But the women interspersed throughout the crowd also looked startlingly alike, with black dresses, hats and veils.

As the clapping died down, Spaulding rose and walked over to a podium in center stage. He spoke into a small microphone, "Welcome to SAINT Special Meeting number 514. We're proud to introduce you to Satch Stevenson, the first Sasquatch to experience a UFO. However, before turning the meeting over to Satch, I've been asked to make a couple of announcements.

"First, Brother Nicodemus announces the grand opening of his new Internal Adjustment Parlor in the rear of Chan Ling's laundry shop on Jackson Street. The first 20 members showing their membership cards to Brother Nicodemus receive 20 percent discounts on joint lubes and pacemaker recharges.

"The other announcement is that Brother Hector has completed construction of his photon-release, hyper drive space van and is now accepting reservations to the regions of Arcturus, Rigel and Alpha Centauri. Sounds like a great way to get away from it all!"

More polite applause filled the hall, along with a few giggles.

"Now, let's hear from our honored guest, Satch Stevenson." Spaulding motioned Satch toward the podium. As the giant Sasquatch rose, the crowd hushed. As Satch strode forward, he pondered the strange announcements, the equally strange clothing of the SAINTS, the rainbow pins and the mechanical motions of the men. Then it struck him. The pieces fell into place like an automated jigsaw puzzle. His face brightened as he realized that tonight his story would be understood and believed.

His talk was interrupted dozens of times with thundering applause and cheers. He told about Major General Huggins' actions and then concluded with, "And I firmly believe that the U.S. Air Force is trying to cover up the facts in this and similar cases."

That comment brought down the house. Wild clapping shot through the hall like volleys of rifle fire. Dozens of members jumped to their feet, yelling, "Right! You know it! Bravo!"

At last, Satch felt like a hero. He bowed, graciously, to the crowd, and while the applause continued several minutes more, he rejoined Spaulding and the Elders.

"I knew they'd believe me," he said, grinning broadly. "But, why didn't you tell me that you're really not humans? I know you've been changed into machines by the Rainbow Race. You see, they told me all about it. They even offered to alter me, but I turned them down. Yes, it finally added up – your rainbow pins, jerky movements, those announcements, even your group's name ... let's see, Saucer Anti-Interference Network Team."

"We don't advertise such facts to strangers," said Spaulding. "People don't often believe us, but when they do, we usually convert them. Our ranks have grown enormously since I was converted in 1389 B.C. You see, I too, met the Rainbow Race, and their offer of Immortality was too great to resist. I was one of the first. Many more followed me in later years. Now, our ranks have swollen to nearly three million members in every major country in the world. It may comfort you to know," concluded Spaulding, "that about three million SAINTS believe you, even though no sinners do."

"Sinners?"

"Yes. Sinners are the skeptics – all those who ridiculed you. But it won't last. You see, as our ranks grow, the numbers of sinners decrease. That's a foregone conclusion – a foregone conclusion," said Spaulding, savoring the words like a juicy steak.

Satch nodded and said, "Well, I'm sure glad that I learned about you. Thanks for inviting me!"

Spaulding smiled, "The pleasure was ours, I assure you."

Around noon the next day, Spaulding's car delivered Satch to the Stevenson house. Marcie picked a half dozen of the plumpest, fuzziest peaches she could spot. Between Satch's chomps and gulps, the pair chatted.

"They believed my story, Marcie."

"Oh, did you tell it a different way?"

"No," replied Satch, "but I did learn more about the total picture. You see, Marcie, there are SAINTS and sinners, and you're not yet a SAINT."

Grinning broadly, Marcie said, "I guess that makes me a sinner. You know, that's what my childhood preacher used to call me when I'd fall asleep during one of his sermons."

Satch expelled the final peach pit against the trunk of a tree, slurped up some runaway juices from his chin and said, "Yeah, Marcie, he was right. But you don't have to stay that way. You see, that guy Spaulding could help you become a SAINT. Then you could live here on Earth, forever, and I know of a Chinese laundry where you could get lubed and recharged, and then, for fun, you could fly to the stars."

Marcie stood there shaking her head while Satch loped off toward home, leaping skyward every so often like a playful puppy. The afternoon air was shattered with a thundering call, "EEE -OOO - WAA!"

About the Author

Lyle Hanson was born on a North Dakota wheat farm and grew up in Enumclaw (Native American for "home of the evil spirits"), Washington. A career teacher in the Lake Washington School District, he spent his youth with boy scouts prowling the rock caves in back of the Weyerhauser Mill near Enumclaw. In "olden days", these rock caves could have provided ample shelter for Sasquatches, and they probably turned the author on to researching and writing about this interesting topic. The present book, "Sasquatch Rainbow School" is the second of a trilogy enjoyed by many of the author's 4th through 6th grade students over the years.